FORTRESS OF BLOOD

BOOK TWO OF THE MINA MURRAY SERIES

LAUREN GOFFIGAN

Copyright © 2017 by Lauren Goffigan

All rights reserved.

This book or any portion thereof may not be reproduced, or stored in a retrieval system, or transmitted in any form or by any means, electronic, mechanical, photocopying, recording, or otherwise, without the express written permission of the publisher.

This is a work of fiction. Names, characters, organizations, places, events, and incidents are either products of the author's imagination or used fictitiously.

Cover Design by Mibl Art

"And you, be ye fruitful, and multiply; bring forth abundantly in the earth, and multiply therein."'

– Genesis 9:7

1
THE ORDER

"No," Anara said, barely containing her fury as she shot to her feet. "Radu has given you the information you need. We will not ally with humans."

I stood in Radu Draculesti's gilded drawing room opposite Anara, with Abraham Van Helsing and Jack Seward hovering behind me. Radu and my half-brother Gabriel were still seated, looking at us with quiet astonishment.

I had just proposed to Radu that we work together to defeat the vampires who had abducted my fiancé, Jonathan Harker . . . vampires that happened to be his biological children. Vlad Draculesti and his sister Ilona were not only responsible for Jonathan's abduction, but other abductions and murders occurring all around Europe as well. We needed to stop them, and the only way to do so was to work together.

I was hardly surprised at Anara's protest—she seemed to hate me the moment she laid eyes on me. Ignoring her protest, I kept my gaze trained firmly on Radu.

"Anara, please," Radu said, frowning at her. "If it were not for my cowardice . . . if I had just forced myself to kill Vlad years ago . . ."

His voice trailed off, dipping with regret, but Anara interrupted him.

"You told me we were done with this fight!"

"I was in denial, my love. I have known that I would one day be forced to confront my children. It seems that day has come. I can no longer close my eyes to what is happening."

Anara vibrated with fury, but she turned and vanished from the room in a flash of movement. The tension dissipated with her departure, and I instantly felt more at ease. Yet I still found it hard to believe that we were even in the presence of vampires—I'd been in denial about their very existence for years.

Only days ago, Abe had approached me on the street in London, and then at a society ball, warning me that the mysterious murders all over Europe were linked to a creature we had encountered in Transylvania—a vampire. I'd refused to believe him; it seemed impossible, but when my fiancé was abducted before my very eyes at the same ball by vampires, I could no longer deny what was happening. We had set out from

London, determined to track down and destroy the creatures who had abducted my fiancé and bring him home.

But along the way, our train had derailed on the way to Transylvania, and in the aftermath, I discovered the existence of my half-brother Gabriel, a human-vampire hybrid whose very existence revealed that my mother kept more secrets than my father ever had. Gabriel had brought us here to Budapest to meet Radu for answers . . . of which he had many.

"Are there others who would be willing to fight with us?" I asked Radu, forcing my mind back to the present. "You told us of a group that was sent to kill Vlad—an order. Who were they?"

Radu was still staring at the doorway, distracted by Anara's departure. It took him several moments to respond.

"Members of the Order of the Dragon," he replied, his dark eyes finally sliding back to mine. "It was an order formed in the Middle Ages. An alliance between ancient vampire families and some trusted humans to maintain order amongst our kind, and to keep our existence hidden from humans. But there has not been an official meeting in over twenty years. After all that has happened, I suspect the surviving members want nothing more to do with the war. But," he added, when my face fell, "there may be some who are still willing to fight. There is someone here in Budapest who may be willing to join us."

"Matyas?" Gabriel asked with a frown. "He loathes humans. He can barely tolerate me."

"He hates Vlad more, and he wants to see him destroyed," Radu replied. Though his tone was calm, it was edged by steel. "He could be a useful ally."

"Who is Matyas?" Seward asked.

"The leader of the vampires here in Budapest," Radu answered. "Like my daughter, he is . . . distrustful of humans. I will need to speak with him before introducing you."

It seemed as if Gabriel wanted to protest, but he remained silent. I was apprehensive at the thought of being introduced to yet another hostile vampire. Anara had nearly killed us. What would this Matyas do?

"I will not allow him to harm you," Radu said, as if reading my mind. "As my guests, he will be expressly forbidden to do so. Matyas may not like humans, but he will not harm you without provocation."

I glanced over at Abe and Seward, who gave me quick nods of assent.

"All right," I agreed.

Radu excused himself to contact Matyas, offering us his guest rooms to rest in until he sent for us.

"Radu and other vampires can fight Vlad on

their own. I can still escort you all back to England," Gabriel said, as he led us out of the drawing room and up the stairs to the guest rooms.

I tensed. I had grown weary of frequently being told to return to England without Jonathan. I opened my mouth to protest, but Seward interjected.

"Don't bother trying to persuade her. I've already made the same suggestion."

"She's not going back to England without Jonathan," Abe added, echoing my earlier statement. "You don't know your sister yet—she can be quite stubborn. Her decision has been made since we left London."

Gabriel frowned, scrutinizing my determined features, but he said nothing.

When we reached the guest rooms on the second floor, Abe asked Gabriel if he could question him further about his abilities while we waited. Abe's scientific curiosity about vampires had only increased since being in direct contact with them, and he looked so comically delighted when Gabriel agreed that Seward and I smiled at each other behind his back, and the earlier friction dissipated.

"You should rest, Abe," I chided, my smile fading as I thought of the injury he had sustained during the train derailment on our journey here. "Your wound still needs—"

"The wound is healing expeditiously," Abe

said, waving off my concerns. "I am fine, Mina. There is no need to worry about me."

They continued down the hall. I was tempted to join them, but fatigue had settled into my limbs like a heavy weight, and I knew I needed to have my wits about me if we were to have a discussion with Matyas.

Like the drawing room, my room was fit for a noble or an aristocrat, with a large bed, a fireplace, and more oriental rugs. I curled up on top of the lush covers of the bed, forcibly clearing my mind of my turbulent thoughts, and I managed to drift off into a restless sleep.

"If you feel you are in danger, leave immediately. I will protect you," Gabriel said to us in a low voice as we all descended the stairs two hours later. I'd just been awoken by Gabriel, and was still groggy from my nap. I had to struggle to concentrate on his words. "Long ago, Matyas' whole family was killed by overzealous humans. He holds human life in no high regard."

"Christ," Seward swore. "Why does Radu think he'll work with us?"

"Because Radu hopes he will put his hatred of humans aside to help destroy Vlad."

To my surprise, Anara was waiting for us at the base of the stairs. She wore a dress of dark purple silk and lace paired with a black cloak, her skin gleaming in the shadowy entrance hall. She looked the part of a mythic creature straight out of some dark fairy tale.

"Come," she said, turning to lead us down the entrance hall to a door at the opposite end. She pushed open the door, and it swung open to reveal a set of stairs leading to a massive cellar. There was a lit lantern perched in a wall holder, and she lifted it out before leading us down the stairs; the light from her lantern casting ominous shadows around the darkened cellar as we entered.

She led us to another door, which opened onto a long winding corridor. I had heard of the extensive cave system that ran beneath the Buda Hills, but I didn't know that they were linked to homes. Though the corridor that lie ahead of us was man made—with its stacked bricks and slots for torches—the ancient underground caves it was carved into had been made by nature.

We entered, walking down the corridor for so long that I became nervous wondering exactly where Anara was taking us, until she abruptly turned into a cavernous room that must have once been a torture chamber with long, rusty metal cages, a fractured wooden rack, and several claw-like metal contraptions chained to its brick walls. It was lit by several ancient torches, which gave the room an eerie glow.

Radu stood in the center of the room, next to

another vampire whom I assumed was Matyas. Matyas was as tall as the other vampires in the room, with pale, angular features and icy blue eyes that gave him the appearance of a wolf in human form. He scrutinized each of us, his cold gaze lingering on me.

Matyas approached us, stopping when he was only a foot away, his lips curling back in a derisive sneer.

"A human woman. You believe that you can defeat Vlad?" he asked, his eyes trained on me, his words tinged with a strange accent that I did not recognize.

"I–I don't think we can defeat him alone," I said, forcing the words past my lips, which had gone stiff with fear. There was a violence that simmered beneath the surface of this vampire—a violence that even Anara didn't possess. "I know that we have the same desire to destroy them. That's why we wish to make an alliance."

"I do not trust humans," Matyas declared, turning back to Radu. "You know this. Their fear rules them; even now I can smell it all over them. I want nothing to do with the fight amongst vampires. It is futile. My followers in the city have already agreed. We have lost too many."

"You said you would consider their request," Radu said tightly.

"Do you not smell their fear? They would not hesitate to turn on us—to take up arms with other humans against us. The human woman can barely contain her fear and hatred for our kind."

"I don't deny that I fear you," I said, desperation forcing the words from my lips. Matyas whirled back to face me, his eyes narrowing as I continued. "Surely, you can't blame me for being fearful of vampires? Vlad killed my father before my very eyes. But my desire to save my fiancé is greater than my fear, I assure you. Just as your hatred for Vlad must be stronger than your hatred for us."

Silence followed my words. Matyas' eyes remained on me for a disconcertingly long moment, but I was becoming accustomed to the long looks of vampires, and I evenly held his gaze.

"I will not join this fight," he repeated, turning from me to address Radu. "Your wayward children are not my concern."

"I accept my responsibility for Vlad—and Ilona," Radu bit out. "But I have wallowed in my regret for too long. They are bringing destruction to both the human and vampire world. Now is the time to end them."

"My decision stands," Matyas said, not at all swayed by Radu's argument.

Radu straightened to his full height, taking a challenging step towards Matyas.

"I will not forget this," he hissed. "You have turned your back on your own kind out of cowardice."

Matyas snarled, a sound that was terrifyingly monstrous, and I instinctively took a step back. The imminent threat of violence in the room was palpable, and Gabriel moved to stand in front of us as Anara hurried to her father's side. Radu didn't flinch as Matyas drew closer to him.

"I am far older and stronger than you. I could kill you where you stand," Matyas seethed. "I will not stand for such insults."

"Matyas," Anara said with forced cordialness, moving forward to step between the two vampires. "We accept your decision. There is no need for *deyaner*."

I did not recognize the strange word, but I noticed that all the vampires in the room froze at its mention. After a tense moment, Matyas backed away from Radu, though his eyes were still raging with fury.

"Leave now or I will not be restrained."

"Radu . . . the decision has been made. Let's take our leave," Anara said, gripping Radu's arm.

Radu glared at Matyas before allowing Anara to lead him from the room. Gabriel ushered us out after them, shadowing us as we left the room. But I chanced one last glance back as we left, and I saw that Matyas was regarding me with an expression alight with a strange sort of . . . recognition.

2

THE LAND BEYOND THE FOREST

"Matyas received the Blood during the height of the witch hunts," Radu said. "He has seen the very worst of human nature, and he cannot look past it."

We had returned from the caverns and now sat gathered around the table in an opulent dining room over a meal of paprika hendl. Radu still looked tense from the confrontation with Matyas, his brow furrowed into an anxious frown.

"Are there are any others who will help us?" Abe asked.

"There is a small fortified village of vampires near Klausenburgh, in Transylvania," Radu said. "Their leader is quite reasonable; she has always been against violence towards humans. If they are still there, I believe they will join us. It would also be a good place for us to prepare for the attack on my son's fortress. If there is time, they can even train you."

"Train the humans?" Anara's words were sharp with incredulity.

"If they are to storm a fortress filled with vampires, they will need to be trained on how to fight them . . . even with other vampires protecting them," Radu replied, unperturbed by her tone. "Who better to train them to fight vampires than vampires themselves?"

"You've already agreed to ally with them," Anara objected. "Now you want to teach them how to destroy us!"

"In this fight we are on the same side, child," Radu said, leveling her with a hard look. "You do not have to join us."

"Radu, I must insist—"

"I will not repeat myself, nor will I argue with you," Radu interrupted. Anara went rigid, and I thought that she would once again storm from the room. Instead, she looked down at the table, folding her shaking hands into her lap.

"There is a village of only vampires? Are there many of these villages?" Abe asked. He was unaffected by the tension between Radu and Anara, and had taken out his journal, furiously scribbling down notes. "How old is Matyas? How old can vampires become?"

"I am aware of at least seven such villages. Vampires who dislike the ruckus of large human populations prefer them. It is easier for us to live in cities without notice, but not in smaller human villages," Radu answered. "Vampires are ageless . . . it is only by force or choice that we die. Matyas is one of the oldest vampires I know. He has nearly four hundred years."

Even though Radu had already indicated Matyas' great age and I had sensed it from the vampire himself, I was still rattled with astonishment. Matyas had been alive since the fifteenth century. I recalled the coldness in his eyes, the immediate distrust when he looked at us. How much human cruelty had he seen over the centuries? How much had he personally experienced? It was no surprise that he did not trust us.

I told Radu about the vampires in the clearing; the strange language they spoke and the fact that they had left me alive.

"The language is our ancient tongue," Radu replied. "I do not know—"

"A language?" Abe interrupted, his eyes going wide as he jotted something down in his journal.

"Long ago, we lived in complete isolation from humans, and we developed our own tongue. There are not many who speak it now that we live among humans—those who do are very old, or have learned it from their elders. I know some words, but my knowledge is not extensive. I do not know why they left you alive, but I am grateful that you were spared."

"What about Ghyslaine?" I asked.

Radu frowned with confusion, and I told him of the word the vampires spoke to me in the clearing, and Vlad's whisper to me on Westminster Bridge.

"I am surprised my son seems to be aware of the word . . . it is not familiar to me," Radu said, still frowning. "I am still young for a vampire, merely in my hundred and tenth year. But an older vampire may recognize it. We will come across them in Transylvania."

A sharp stab of disappointment pierced me at his response. I had so many questions and was hungry for answers, especially this particular one; I knew there had to be some crucial information I was missing. Ghyslaine, whatever the word meant, had to be a vital clue.

Despite my lack of an appetite, I forced myself to eat, first taking a sip of the slivovitz—a sweet sort of brandy Gabriel told me was made from plums. The meal was as delicious as it smelled, and my stomach rumbled in satisfied appreciation when I began to eat.

During the meal, Gabriel told us how he met Radu and Anara. He had come to Budapest for a visit several years ago, wanting to explore the ancient caves rumored to exist beneath the city, and found himself cornered by a hostile Matyas and several of his followers in an isolated part of the Castle District. Matyas had the ability to sense unfamiliar vampires who arrived in the city. He was immediately suspicious of Gabriel, as hybrids were exceedingly rare. Radu had come to Gabriel's defense, shielding him from Matyas' rancor by offering to host him as his guest, and he allowed Gabriel to stay with him whenever he visited the city.

I looked at Anara, who was absently sipping the slivovitz, lost in her own thoughts, and I wondered how Radu had come to meet her. They weren't biological father and daughter, so he must have been the one to turn her into vampire. But under what circumstances? Anara looked up and met my eyes, as if discerning what I was thinking, and I swiftly looked away.

"You should all sleep," Radu said, as our meal concluded. "We are to take the early morning train to Klausenburgh tomorrow."

But back in my guest room, I could not sleep. I crawled out of bed and sat down at the reading table, opening one of Abe's journals that I had borrowed in order to read some of the notes he'd taken.

Vampiric Abilities: Speed, enhanced hearing, visual prowess, esp at night. Great strength. Reduced / no aging (need to clarify) / does not die natural causes . . . immortal. Some—hypnosis, paralysis, telepathy. They call it 'thrall'. Mind reading? Linked to telepathy? (Need to confirm)

Weaknesses: Needs to consume blood to

survive . . . no longer than two weeks, perhaps longer? Some—sensitive to light. Can only die when staked through the heart, otherwise injured but heal. Beheading also works. Other ways to kill unknown. Comparable species—wolves, possibly feline animals. <u>Common descent possible</u>?

Note: need more info on Eva Murray, Mina's mother.

I froze at the mention of my mother, but turned the page and kept reading.

How is Gabriel's birth possible? Must be others like him. Note: Vampires able have biological children as well as "create" children i.e. Subjects Radu / Anara. But Mina's mother human. <u>How possible???</u>

I set down the journal on the table and wearily closed my eyes. Beneath the remnants of shock I had felt since learning of Gabriel's existence, that same question had been fluttering about in my mind like a restless bird. There must be others like Gabriel, vampires born to human mothers. How many were there? Did some of them turn feral, or were they as kind and human-like as Gabriel? Did they have the ability to turn others into creatures like them? Or did they reproduce as humans did, creating more half-vampire children in the process? These questions were still in my mind as I fell asleep.

∽

We departed from Radu's home early the next morning. It was strange and surreal to travel with vampires, watching them take their seats on the train amongst other humans who had no idea they were traveling with creatures of lore. Had I inadvertently ridden the Underground with vampires in London, or in my previous travels across the continent? Had I passed by them on the streets? Paid them no mind as I went about the monotony of my days?

"It's odd, isn't it?" Seward whispered to me, clearly sharing my thoughts as the train pulled away from the station. Radu, Anara, and Gabriel sat behind us, and I could feel the chill of their cold eyes on my skin. "A few days ago I couldn't even say the word 'vampire'. And now . . ."

"I don't know if I will ever get used to the knowledge," I quietly agreed.

"At Scotland Yard, the inspector I trained under taught me a method," Seward said. "A method that's become handy. He urged me to not dismiss any possibility when it came to solving a crime—not unless it could be disproven."

"But some things can't be disproven," I said with a frown, thinking of some of the experiments Father had performed.

"Well, that's just it," Seward replied with a shrug. "With what I was seeing, I couldn't bloody well disprove that vampires were killing those people. And because I couldn't, I didn't dismiss it.

I wanted to; the very notion was absurd. But the more I investigated the Ripper murders, and from my conversations with Abe, I knew there was no other explanation. Now look where we are," he said, shaking his head in a daze and gesturing towards the vampires seated all around us. "Surrounded by them. And you're related to one."

He gave me a wry smile, and I made myself return it, though I still felt uneasy as my gaze found Gabriel in the back of the train.

Our train pulled into the Klausenburgh station just before noon. Abe took a cab to the post office to pick up the weapons the gunsmith had shipped from Amsterdam, before meeting up with us at the stables on the outskirts of town.

At the stables, the stableman seemed to know Radu quite well, giving him a warm smile and embrace as he spoke to him in rapid German. He provided us with several horses, and we were soon riding out of Klausenburgh and into the surrounding countryside, crossing the wide expanse of the Somes Plateau, until we entered the ancient forests that seemed to dominate much of Transylvania.

The same strong sense of nostalgia that had swept over me in Amsterdam affected me once more, but this nostalgia brought back far darker memories.

Transylvania seemed to belong on a continent of its own, with its vast wilderness of forests, isolated lakes, streams and caverns, and the ever-present shadow of the Carpathians looming in the distance. Death seemed to abide here, something the locals seemed to embrace rather than shy away from with their religious rituals. There was the *parastas,* a memorial service held forty days after the deceased was buried to celebrate the soul's departure to heaven; the eve of All Souls Day, when family graves were cleaned and candles lit to honor the dead; and the strange tradition of holding a *nunta mortilor*, a wedding of the dead for a deceased person who had died unmarried.

And then there were the superstitions. The whispered rumors of witches, pixies, and hobgoblins that hid in the forests, ready to do harm to any humans who crossed their path. Father, Abe and I used to come across protective crosses on homes and wreaths of garlic hung in doorways to ward off supernatural evil. Vampires, the monsters in human skin who roamed the night, was the most pervasive rumor.

Emerging from my reverie, I took in the vaguely familiar sights of the Transylvanian countryside. Every once in a while, we passed the crumbled ruins of some medieval castle off in the distance; Saxon towns, villages, fortified churches and farms otherwise dotted the landscape. But the region seemed more deserted than it had been when I first visited—many of the towns and villages we passed were now empty or sparsely populated. I wondered morbidly if this was what the rest of Europe would become. The world. Completely deserted as the population was killed, abducted, or fled.

My hands were trembling on my reins when we arrived at a fortified village sometime later. A high stone wall and several watchtowers surrounded the village on all sides, while a massive gate dominated its entrance. As our horses trotted towards the gate, Radu held up his hand.

"Please remain here," he said, addressing me, Abe and Seward.

We obligingly lingered behind while Radu, Anara, and Gabriel rode towards the gate. As soon as they dismounted, the gate swung open.

The woman who hurried out enveloped Radu in a warm embrace. She was petite with honey colored skin and fine features framed by a long cascade of dark wavy hair, and her eyes were a vivid mixture of green, brown, and gold. She turned to look at us, and I felt the unmistakable chill of a vampire's gaze. I saw a brief flicker of recognition in her eyes as she studied me, but it quickly dissipated.

Behind her, dozens of men and women approached the gate, looking both delighted and relieved to see Radu. Radu turned and gestured for us to follow them inside, and we dismounted from our horses, heading through the gate and into the central courtyard.

A white steepled gothic hall church overlooked the large courtyard, which was dotted with a patchwork of vegetable gardens. Saxon-style homes with thatched roofs lined the inner fortress wall, alongside storage cells that had been strategically built into the wall.

I looked around at the people gathered in the courtyard, counting nearly fifty humans—and some vampires, I suspected. From their attire, I deduced that most of the humans were Romani; the women wore the traditional dress of colorful ankle-length skirts paired with aprons and scarves covering their hair, while the men wore hats, vests over their long-sleeved shirts, and boots. There seemed to be no obvious tension between the humans and vampires; they seemed unified, and we were the outsiders.

"Both the Romani and vampires have been persecuted by humans," Gabriel said softly. He stood at my side, and had noted my surprise. "Vampires have protected them, and they have shielded vampires in turn."

The female vampire introduced herself as Szabina and ushered us into the church, which was filled with rows of wooden pews, its high-vaulted ceiling making the small interior seem larger and more imposing. We sat in the front pews while the other humans and vampires crowded behind us and in the aisles.

Radu addressed Szabina and the others in

Romanian. I didn't speak the language, but I assumed he was giving them a brief overview of our journey and our intention to get to the fortress to kill Vlad, and rescue Jonathan along with the other prisoners.

As Radu spoke, Szabina's eyes strayed to me. Though her countenance remained neutral, it seemed oddly probing. Did she know me somehow? When I met her gaze full on, Szabina averted her eyes, returning her focus to Radu.

"Vlad and Ilona's vampires have attacked near the human villages," she said, speaking in heavily accented English for our benefit, when Radu had finished. "Those who have not been abducted or murdered have fled to the cities. Those who remain have joined those monsters out of fear. This is one of the few villages they have not attacked. They know vampires dwell here. But soon, they will come."

"Then time is of great importance," Radu said urgently. "Will you join us?"

"I do not think the humans should attempt to fight them," Szabina said, once again glancing at me.

"The humans will fight. They have come too far not to," Radu said, before we could protest. "They have already survived two attacks by ferals. If you and the others are willing, they can be trained."

"We tried fighting back against them," Szabina

said, with quiet desperation. "It is why our numbers are low. We have lost many in the fight. We tried riding out to villages for others to fight with us, but no one is left. Whatever Vlad's plan is ... he is winning."

A grave silence fell, and my body grew cold with dread. The villagers back in Ijsbran had refused to join us, then Matyas, and now Szabina. Even with Radu, Anara, and Gabriel, how could we hope to attack the fortress if Vlad had hundreds of followers at his disposal? We could not attack on our own.

"His plan is to invade. You must know that by now," I said, getting to my feet to face Szabina and all who were gathered. "Our numbers are not great, but we can still fight. What is the alternative? To let them take over? To let them win? You say other villagers have fled. One day soon, there may be nowhere to flee to. We have no choice but to try to stop Vlad. We must."

As Szabina translated my words, I met the eyes of every human and vampire gathered around the church. The gazes that met mine ranged from caution, to wariness, to hope.

"You know she speaks the truth, Szabina," Radu said, when Szabina had finished translating.

"She does," Szabina replied, her eyes holding mine for a long moment. "But I will leave the choice up to the villagers."

She turned to face the others and spoke in

hushed Romanian. I stood nervously as the humans and vampires began speaking amongst themselves. Finally, several men and women turned to Szabina, giving her an affirming nod.

"Very well, Mina," Szabina said, not meeting my eyes. "They have decided. We will fight one last time."

3

TRAINING

We took a midday meal in one of the larger homes that lined the fortress wall, where we ate ghiveci—a hearty vegetable stew—and bread. Szabina, Radu, and a few of the curious human villagers joined us as we ate. Szabina and Radu remained in a corner of the large kitchen, speaking to each other in hushed tones. Szabina glanced over at me periodically, her expression tumultuous. I was increasingly convinced that she knew me somehow, and made a mental note to ask her when I had the chance.

But in the meanwhile, I ignored Szabina's frequent glances, focusing on one of the few English-speaking villagers, a young woman named Elisabeta, who sat with us. She had a cascade of dark curly hair and warm brown eyes, and she kindly answered our questions about the village. She told us that fortified villages such as this one were built in medieval times as a place of refuge for villagers during prolonged sieges and attacks. Such villages now provided a much-needed sanctuary, given the recent rash of vampire attacks.

"My people weak to the attacks—we live on outskirts of villages. Szabina saved our life when our village attacked. She gave us shelter."

"Weren't you afraid of them?" Seward asked.

"We always known of the *strigoi*. Szabina is good. She one of us long ago. *Strigoi* who attacked —they not like Szabina or Radu. Their eyes black . . . their souls gone. Those *strigoi* we fear," she added, with a shiver.

"We need to prepare," Radu interrupted, moving away from Szabina to take a seat at the far end of our table. "The fortress needs to be thoroughly scouted before we can make an accurate plan of attack. I am having two scouts ride ahead, which gives us a full day and a half to ready ourselves until they return. Szabina and the other vampires here will help train you."

Soon after our meal, Szabina gathered all the humans who were to fight in the central courtyard, ordering us to bring our weapons with us. Anara, Radu, Gabriel, and several other vampires moved to stand in an intimidating row in front of us.

Despite her petite stature, I could tell that Szabina commanded much respect; she held everyone's attention as she stepped forward, her multicolored eyes continually straying towards me as she addressed us in Romanian, and then English.

"We are strong and we are fast. Many of us can hold our prey in thrall," Szabina said, her voice carrying across the courtyard. "But we do have weaknesses. We can be staked or beheaded. Aim for here, or here," she said, pointing to her heart, and then her throat. "Anywhere else may wound us, but not kill. For the thrall, avoid looking in the eyes . . . that is how we enter your mind."

She stopped speaking for a moment, allowing her words to settle. Next to me, Seward and Abe listened intently, and I could practically see Abe sorting the information in his mind to be added to his journal later.

"Make certain you have your weapons. None of us will harm you, but the vampires at Vlad's fortress will try to rip you apart," she concluded darkly.

I held one of my kukri knives in my left hand; the second one and a knife were securely stowed in my sleeves and the bodice of my dress. Around me, the other humans clutched knives and makeshift wooden stakes. Abe and Seward stood at my side. Seward had lost his revolver in the train derailment, and was now armed with two of Abe's knives.

Szabina nodded to the other vampires, and

they moved into predatory crouches. Though I knew they would not harm us, apprehension filled me at the sight. Even Radu and Gabriel, whom I had slowly come to trust, looked lethal in their crouched positions.

Szabina did not give us the order to run; she and the other vampires merely sprang towards us at an impossibly fast speed.

My instincts set in, and I turned on my heel to race towards the open gates and out of the village, dashing into the depths of the surrounding forest with the other humans.

Seward, Abe, and I kept pace together as we ran, but a vampire soon tackled Seward to the ground from behind, while another grabbed Abe and slammed him against a tree.

I halted when the vampire grabbed Abe, raising my kukri to intervene, but Abe's eyes met mine as he struggled with the vampire.

"Run, Mina!" he shouted.

I had to remind myself that this was a training exercise; they would not harm Abe. But I was still fearful as I raced away from him.

I only made it a few yards when a hand gripped my neck and pinned me down to the ground from behind. But the grip was gentle, and I twisted around to see Gabriel hovering above me.

"You need to fight me, Mina," he said. "You can wound me. I will heal."

I tried to yank myself out of his grip, but he was far too strong. I turned back to look at him, hesitant. My growing trust made me reluctant to wound him; I could not believe that I'd nearly killed him only two days ago.

Seeing my continued hesitation, Gabriel yanked my head backward, more roughly this time, and bared his teeth. At the sight, my instincts took over, and I swiftly sank my kukri back into his shoulder. Gabriel let out a howl of pain, loosening his grip, and I stumbled to my feet to scramble away.

The trees whipped past me as I ran, and through the forest depths I could vaguely hear frantic shouts and cries as the other humans fought off the vampires. But the sounds became more distant as I ran, and I soon found myself in a dark patch of forest.

The trees grew closer together here, their density allowing very little sunlight to filter through their coiled branches—a dark prison erected by nature. A sense of dread crept over me, and I turned to race back towards the village.

But as soon as I turned, I heard a vicious snarl from the black depths of the forest behind me, and felt the cold gaze of a vampire. Had I stumbled across a random feral roaming through the countryside? Had I strayed too far from the others?

I started to dash out of the clearing, lifting up

my skirt to pick up my speed, but when I heard the swift cracking of twigs and snapping of branches behind me, I knew the vampire was racing towards me and would soon overtake me. I continued to run, opening my mouth to let out a desperate scream to alert the others.

A cold hand reached out and gripped me by my neck from behind, as Gabriel had done only moments earlier, abruptly cutting off my scream. This time, the hold was far rougher than my brother's grip had been.

My captor yanked me around. It was Anara, but I felt no relief at the sight of her; her eyes were ferocious and filled with the promise of violence.

She dropped her hand from my throat. Her gaze remained trained on mine as my body lifted from the ground, and I was slammed hard against a nearby tree. Unable to move, terror flooded me as Anara stalked towards me like a wolf approaching fresh prey. When she reached me, her hand again went to my throat, her eyes burning like fire. Her hand tightened around my throat and I panicked as I struggled to breathe.

We were completely alone in the clearing, and her face showed no hint of mercy as she continued to squeeze the air from my lungs. I had no way to defend myself, no way to fight back.

I did not know why Anara hated me so, but even with her hand on my throat, I knew instinctively that she wasn't evil. There was more to her, a pain and humanity that was absent from the mindless ferals I had encountered. I raised my eyes to hers in desperation, pleading with my eyes for her to release me. But when my eyes locked with hers . . . something strange happened. I saw something. Felt something.

I was a young girl, my reed thin arms wrapped around my legs as I wept and rocked myself back and forth, seated in the center of the splintered wooden floor of a tiny cottage that had been ransacked; furniture and scraps of food were scattered about. In front of me, a man and a woman—my parents?—were being dragged away by a group of men.

"Please! Don't harm my little girl!" the woman screamed. Her pain was palpable; her body wracked with grief and terror. "Leave my Anara be! Please, she has done nothing! I beg you!"

"Take me, please!" the man begged. "Leave my wife and child alone. Kill me, not them! Please!"

"Mama!" I screamed. The word was thin and my throat was strained, as if I had been crying for days. I scrambled to my feet and raced towards my parents. "Papa!"

One of the men stepped forward and backhanded me, sending me sailing across the room, and I hit the wall with such force that I slipped from consciousness.

And then the scene was gone. I was back in the present, crouched on my hands and knees on the ground, coughing and gasping for breath. Anara had stumbled away from me, her hands pressed to the sides of her head, looking dazed.

I was disoriented by what I had seen, but my self-preservation kept me focused, and I reached for the kukri that had dropped to the ground, holding it out defensively should she try to attack me again.

But Anara made no move towards me, her eyes clouded with confusion as she looked at me, her breathing ragged. We stood at a stalemate for several moments, until I dimly heard multiple footfalls approach the clearing.

"Mina!" Abe shouted as he raced into the clearing, his eyes sweeping over me with fretfulness. "I heard you scream. Are you—"

"I'm . . . I'm all right," I said hastily, as other humans and vampires began to file into the clearing.

Gabriel hurried into the clearing, pushing past the others, his gaze straying suspiciously from me to Anara. When he saw my throat, he grabbed Anara and pinned her to a tree, his lips curled back in a ferocious snarl.

"Did you harm my sister?" he roared.

But Anara was unfazed by Gabriel's fury. She was still focused on me, her confused expression shifting to one of suspicion.

"How did you do that?" she demanded,

ignoring Gabriel. "You were in my mind. You did something to me!"

"You are far stronger and she's the one who is bruised! Answer me!" Gabriel shouted.

"What is happening?" Szabina asked sharply. She and Radu entered the clearing, moving past the cluster of humans and vampires who had gathered.

"She attacked my sister!" Gabriel snapped.

"Anara. I already warned you—" Radu began, looking furious.

"I–I wasn't going to kill her! She was able to release herself from the thrall, which is impossible!" Anara cried, pointing a quivering finger at me. "She was in my mind. I felt her!"

Szabina stiffened at her words, and I saw alarm flicker in her eyes.

"Harming the humans is forbidden," Szabina said, disregarding Anara's words, her voice strained.

"You are dismissed from the training," Radu added. "I will discuss this with you later. Please escort her back to the village," he quietly ordered two hovering vampires, who approached Anara.

"Listen to me! She looked at me, I felt something in my mind, and I could no longer hold her in thrall. No human has ever done that to me before!" Anara cried fervently, as the two vampires gripped her arms to lead her away.

But Radu and Szabina didn't look at her, and

once she was gone, Szabina approached, studying me closely.

"Is that true?" she asked. "You released yourself from the thrall?"

A hush fell as Abe, and all the others who were gathered, turned curious and awestruck looks towards me. I flushed, suddenly feeling oddly defensive, as if I had done something wrong.

"I–I just looked into her eyes, and I saw—I think I saw something from Anara's childhood. It was like a dream. Or a memory. Her parents were being dragged away."

Radu went rigid at my words, frowning. The silence stretched.

"Perhaps it was my desperation," I said hastily, unable to bear the silence or the strange looks the others were giving me. "If one of you can put me into another thrall, I can show you all what I did, and then—"

"No," Gabriel interjected. "It is too dangerous, and there's no guarantee you will be able to release yourself again."

"We need to learn to defend ourselves against the thrall! It's one of your most powerful weapons," I protested. "If I can teach others to do what I just did, our chances against Vlad and his followers are even greater."

"I agree with Gabriel," Abe said, looking worried. "It is far too dangerous."

"My daughter was right," Radu spoke up,

looking at me intently. "We are not aware of any other human who has been able to release themselves from the thrall. Others here may not be able to do the same."

Tendrils of unease curled around me as everyone continued to look at me like I was a newly discovered specimen. What did it mean that I was able to break the thrall? Yet another question to add to the mountain of unknowns.

"We are losing time. Let us take a break from the training," Szabina said. "We meet back in the courtyard."

Everyone began to scatter, casting curious glances at me as they did so. Abe, Seward, and Gabriel approached me, and beneath their polite urgings for me to get some rest, I could see the inquisitiveness in their eyes at this newly discovered ability of mine.

I barely listened to their words. My focus was on Szabina, who remained at the edge of the clearing, watching me with turbulent eyes, before she turned to head back towards the village.

"Are you listening?" Abe asked impatiently. "I want to examine your neck to see if there—"

"Wait here," I said shortly, leaving them behind as I hurried after Szabina. I was determined to find out the cause of her frequent looks.

She seemed to sense that I was following her, as she picked up her pace. Worried that she would use her vampiric speed to evade me, I quickly jogged forward to move in front of her, blocking her path.

"You keep looking at me. Why?" I demanded.

When Szabina stiffened, averting her eyes, I knew that my inkling was correct. She knew something, and for whatever reason, she was hiding it from me.

"Szabina, please. Do you know something about me?" I pressed. "There is so much that I don't know about my own past, my own life. If you know something, please . . ." my voice broke, and I had to blink back my tears.

Compassion flared in her eyes, and she expelled a long breath.

"I did not want to believe it at first . . . I still cannot," she said. "But I have only seen one human break the thrall of a vampire, and I have lived many years. Do you know the name Ghyslaine?"

I froze as my heart began to pummel against my ribcage. Ghyslaine. It did mean something—something vital. I could see it in her eyes. And she knew my connection to it.

I felt a sudden and strange sense of stillness; like the calm right before a violent storm. I had felt it right before Gabriel revealed his identity, and the night that I stumbled into that clearing to find my father's dead body. It was the sense that everything would soon change, and my world would not be the same.

Szabina's vivid eyes were now shimmering with blood tears. She stepped forward, placing cold trembling hands on the side of my face, gazing at me with a look of near reverence.

"Wilhelmina Murray," Szabina whispered. "I know who you are."

4

GHYSLAINE

"*Once upon a time, there lived a little girl,*" *my mother whispered.*

I was five years old, seated with my legs tucked beneath me on my bed. It was night, long past my bedtime, but I was wide awake. My mother sat next to me, her eyes distant as she lovingly stroked my hair. The moonlight that filtered in my bedroom window gave her face an eerie glow.

"What was her name?" I asked eagerly.

"Isabel," Mother replied, after a long pause. "Isabel was the youngest daughter of a family that killed monsters."

"Monsters?" I whispered, my hands flying to my mouth. "What kind of monsters?"

"Monsters that look like us. Only they take blood. They take life," Mother replied, her eyes

going dark. "But Isabel's family realized that not all these monsters are evil."

"But monsters are evil!" I objected.

"Not so, poppet," Mother said, with a small smile that was more sad than amused. "Many of them could not help that they were monsters. They never harmed humans . . . they only wanted to live in peace. Isabel's family stopped hunting them, and much time passed. But many of the bad monsters remembered the family. They hunted them down. One by one, all the family members were killed, until there was only one left alive."

I drew my knees up to my chest, wrapping my arms around my legs. I usually liked Mother's stories, but this one was frightening. Yet I still wanted to know more.

"Who was left?" I asked nervously.

"A little girl named Wilhelmina," Mother replied, pinching my nose affectionately. I giggled, turning my head away. Mother fell silent once more, her hand dropping to the blanket, her eyes growing distant once more. "Wilhelmina was the only one left, but she did not know it. It was best that she did not know, because if the monsters knew about her, they would come after her. But they will not," she added reassuringly, noticing my alarm. "Because she was hidden away in the biggest city of the human world with a different name; impossible to find. She was . . . she was safe. She lived a long *and happy life, away from the monsters and darkness."*

In the faint light, I thought I saw a shimmer of tears in her troubled brown eyes.

"Mama, is this just a story?" I asked.

"Of course, poppet," she swiftly replied, reaching out to gently cup my chin with a consoling smile. But there was a strain to the smile, and her hand trembled slightly on my face. "Just a story."

I now recalled the story as I stumbled through the forest outside of the village, hot tears staining my cheeks. Behind me, I could feel both Abe and Gabriel's concerned gazes on my back as they trailed me. I stopped to lean heavily against a tree, closing my eyes against a fresh rush of tears.

The story my mother told me all those years ago had not been a mere bedtime story.

IN THE STUNNED wake that followed Szabina's words, she gently led me back to the church, sitting me down in the front pew. I was still reeling, and barely noticed as she politely ushered out the few humans who were congregated inside until we were alone. She must have sent for the others, because Gabriel, Abe, Seward, and Radu soon joined us. Szabina moved to the altar, gesturing for Gabriel to sit next to me in the front pew.

"Ghyslaine is your mother's family name," she said somberly, her eyes trained on the both of us.

I blinked at her in confusion. I did not quite know what I was expecting, but it wasn't this.

"No," I said, shaking my head. "My mother's maiden name was Smith."

"That was the name she took when she left France for England," Szabina replied. "Eva Smith. She changed it to protect her identity. Her name was Isabel Ghyslaine."

The blood drained from my face. Aside from Abe's sharp intake of breath behind me, the church was still and silent.

"The Ghyslaines were once a noble family who learned of vampires before most humans," Szabina spoke slowly and softly, as if keenly aware of the weight of each word. "They were already brutal and efficient witch hunters. They were often ordered by royalty to lead the hunts. But there are no witches . . . there have not been for ages. They discovered vampires through their hunts, and the Ghyslaine family massacred scores of vampires. They soon stopped—no one knows why—but they were so hated by our kind that when they began to lose their lands and decline in power, their descendants were hunted down and killed. Many changed their names and went into hiding. Your mother belonged to possibly the last family of descendants. But her family . . . they were good. They were ashamed of the family's legacy and protected vampires rather than hunt them. Your grandfather was a member of the Order of the Dragon. When he died, your mother took his place. I was a member as well; that is how I came to know her. She was a good person."

I couldn't move nor speak, and I was forced into a shocked stillness for several moments.

"She . . . she was ill. She died at sea when she left to get treatment," I whispered when I was able to find words. I was still struggling to hold on to some threads of truth that I had always known, threads that were now slipping through my fingers. "I–I saw her sick in her bed. Father showed me the headline about the boat sinking; the ticket she purchased. I . . . we held a funeral."

"She needed to use deceit in order to leave. She was very involved in the fight against Vlad. She was one of the members who attempted to kill him. She hoped that she could kill Vlad and return home to her children. She did not want you to know any of this—not even your father knew," Szabina whispered, guilt darting across her expression. "She made me vow to never tell of her fate should she be killed in the fight. I never thought I would meet you. I still cannot believe I stand opposite her children."

"What of my father?" Gabriel bit out. "Who was he?"

"I do not know. She kept that secret. She insisted that he was dead."

"How did she die?" I whispered.

"She was one of the members of the Order killed in retaliation for his death. I am so sorry," she said mournfully, her eyes once again glistening with a sheen of blood tears. "We tried to protect the ones who fought Vlad, but his followers were fiercely loyal, angry, and determined. They got to her before we could stop them."

Gabriel buried his face in his hands and began to weep. I suspected my mother's death had been a great burden for him; he'd known and remembered her more than I did, and he'd been forced to mourn her death from afar, to shoulder it all on his own. My hand seemed to reach out of its own accord to grip one of his hands, and his hand tightened over mine as he continued to weep.

Grief felt somewhat lighter when it was shared, and I felt a sense of solidarity with Gabriel because of it. Any lingering doubt or unease about what he was had completely dissipated. In that moment, we were just two orphaned children, sharing the heavy weight of parental loss. Everyone else in the church was silent, allowing us this moment to grieve.

In the long silence, memories seized my thoughts. I was once again a five-year-old child, hovering in the doorway of Mother's bedroom while a nurse tended to her, her sad eyes trained on me. And then she was hovering above me as I tried to sleep, her anguished face glowing in the moonlight, making her appear ethereal and dream like. *I must leave. But never forget my love for you, poppet. I love you always.* Father was kneeling down next to me, brushing my hair back from my face, his voice wavering as he spoke. *Your mother has gone away to get well. She will be better when she returns.* The solemn funeral on that rainy October day, Father's hand clutching mine, the rain mingling with the tears on my cheeks.

"How did they kill her?" I asked suddenly, forcing the ugly question past my lips.

"Mina," Abe's concerned voice was behind me, close to my ear, his hand reaching out to rest on my shoulder. "There's no need—"

"I've been kept in the dark for too long," I interrupted. "I need to know."

"As do I," Gabriel whispered, looking pained.

"Mina," Szabina said, shaking her head. "I do not think—"

"Tell us. We are her children. We deserve to know."

"She was in hiding in a house in the German countryside," Szabina said, hesitant. "It was a brief stay . . . just until it was safe for her to return home. She did not want to risk vengeful vampires following her back to London. But Vlad's followers found her. When we got to her, it was too late. She looked . . . she looked as if she had been tortured. Her body had been drained of blood. We knew we could not send her body back to England, Robert would know that she had not died natural. On the day your mother left England, a ship sank in the Channel; many bodies were lost at sea. We . . . we arranged—" Szabina faltered, lowering her eyes, guilt lurking in their depths, "a forged ticket in her name, and sent a letter to your father telling him that she was on the boat—and her body was lost at sea. We buried her in France with others of her family."

I closed my eyes. I had wanted to know how she died, needed to know, but the circumstances of her death were even more horrible than I could comprehend. I felt no anger towards Szabina for her actions in hiding the true nature of Mother's death—it was clear that it had been Mother's wish. Instead, I only felt a strange numbness. Everything I believed about myself was false; I was heir to a dark legacy that I could no longer deny.

Without a word, I got to my feet and walked out of the church, ignoring Abe as he called after me. Both Abe and Gabriel trailed me as I continued through the central courtyard, past the two vampires who stood guard by the village gate, and into the forest.

Now, they hovered behind me as the numbness dissipated and I began to weep. I wept for my parents, who had both died at the hands of vampires. For my years of ignorance. For Jonathan, whose fate I desperately feared for.

But I did feel an odd sense of completion.

The gaps in my knowledge of the past were filled, and I no longer desired my previous ignorance. I felt like a blind woman who had just received the gift of sight after wandering for years in the dark. For the first time, I truly knew who I was and what I had to do. The sudden surge of determination that swelled in my chest was so strong that it overpowered my other tumultuous emotions, and a sort of calm settled over me.

I straightened, wiping away my tears, turning to face Abe and Gabriel. Gabriel still looked grief-stricken, his eyes glistening with tears, while Abe's face was heavy with worry.

"I have an idea," I whispered.

"My mother was able to release herself from the thrall, was she not?" I asked Szabina. "She's the one you were referring to."

We had returned to the church, where Szabina and Radu had remained, speaking quietly to each other. Seward still sat in his pew, looking dazed from the latest revelations. He rose from his seat as we entered.

"Yes," Szabina replied. "She was the only human I knew who could do such a thing. It made her invaluable in the fight against Vlad."

"Vlad and his followers hate the Ghyslaine

family and it appears many of them somehow know that I'm a descendant."

"You have the look of your mother, and some vampires can smell it in your blood," Szabina replied with a nod.

"They can smell her ancestry in her blood?" Abe asked, intrigued.

"Yes. Every human has a smell—from their skin, their blood. Families share similar smells. It is not common, but some vampires do have a greater sense of smell than others; it can be passed on to other vampires they create."

"Is it possible that I'm one of the last descendants of this Ghyslaine family?" I asked Szabina, trying to keep my voice steady as I drew everyone's focus back to me. There was no time for Abe's scientific musings about the vampiric sense of smell. Not with what I was planning.

"Yes," Szabina acknowledged.

"Then when we attack the fortress, I should be used as bait to draw them out," I continued. "It may be the best way we have of entering."

"No!" Gabriel protested. "After what we have just learned, how can you even think of—"

"Nothing has changed, Gabriel. I'm now even more desperate to rescue Jonathan—and avenge our mother and my father. We must find a way in without a massive loss of life. We don't have the numbers to just charge forward. If their focus is on me, they will send their forces out and give the rest of you the time you need to enter. Once we have them scattered—"

"We can enter the fortress in waves and attack," Radu said, completing my thought.

"Radu," Gabriel breathed. "You're not—"

"Mina is right," Radu interrupted. "We do need a way to lower their defenses. It is what I have been discussing with the others. We have already considered using some of the human villagers as bait if they are willing. Are you certain about this, Mina?"

"Yes." There was no hesitation in my voice, though dread stirred in my stomach at the thought, dread that I quickly pushed aside. I had to do whatever it took to get Jonathan away from those monsters.

Gabriel moved to stand in front of me, gripping my shoulders, his desperate eyes searching mine.

"Our mother didn't want us to know about any of this," he said. "Your father never wanted you to return to Transylvania. If you put yourself in Vlad's path, you are defying what they—"

"What would you have me do? Go back to London and let these creatures take over Europe and the rest of the world? My parents' secrets didn't keep me, nor anyone safe. It only prolonged the inevitable. I will no longer hide from this. I must do what I can to destroy Vlad and save my fiancé. Stop trying to dissuade me!"

Gabriel dropped his hands from my shoulders, his face turbulent.

"I know you made a promise to her, Gabriel. But I must do this. I'm doing this for our mother—for all of us. I'm finishing what she started. Please understand," I said, my tone softening.

Gabriel's eyes darkened and he took a step back from me.

"I have failed her," he whispered, turning to leave the church.

"I will discuss this new plan with the others. Everyone will need to know their roles," Radu said after Gabriel's abrupt departure. Szabina nodded, giving me a long look before she and Radu filed out of the church.

Abe, Seward, and I were now alone. I sank back down into the pew, staring dully out of the windows which illuminated the interior of the church with the fading light of the sun. Abe and Seward were silent, but I could feel their gazes on my skin.

"If you're going to try to change my mind—" I began, turning to face them.

"We know better," Seward interjected, giving me a small smile. "I'm going to see what I can do to help the others. I'll leave you alone."

Abe lingered for a moment before following Seward, and I sat alone in the stillness of the church. I thought of my mother, Isabel Ghyslaine, the mysterious and shadowy figure from my early childhood, who had now taken on a fully formed image in my mind. She had been brave, strong, loyal, and loving. How had she managed to keep so many secrets? To know of the dark world of vampires that lurked unnoticed in the midst of humans, an invisible storm cloud that hovered above the entire world. How isolated she must have felt towards the end of her life, to bear such a secret alone. She had a brief taste of normalcy and happiness with her children and her husband, before it was snatched from her. The tragedy of her short life and death suddenly hit me with a force so strong that I keeled over in the pew, wrapping my arms around my body.

I closed my eyes against the tears that rose, sharply blinking them away. The time for tears had passed. My mother's burden had become my own, and after years of ignorance, it was time for me to complete what Isabel Ghyslaine had set out to do with the other members of the Order of the Dragon. Destroy Vlad Alexandru Draculesti, and those that followed him.

5

MONSTERS AND DARKNESS

I dashed through the thicket of trees, their branches whipping past as I hurtled by. Behind me, several vampires gave chase, rapidly closing in on me. I skidded to a stop as I reached a small clearing, where Szabina was waiting, crouched in the familiar stance of attack.

Trying to steady my breathing, I raised my kukri, but Szabina lunged forward before I could, pinning me down beneath her as she bared her elongated fangs. A strangled scream caught in my throat as she leaned in close, her fangs a mere inch from my throat.

She released me, springing back to her feet as she looked down at me with grave disappointment.

"You are dead," she said wearily. "Mina, you are not using your instincts."

I struggled to my feet, discouraged. Though this was just a training session, the chase had left me shaken. Szabina and the other vampires had been training me for hours now, and I could feel the heat of the midday sun penetrating the thick shade of trees, heating my flushed and sweating skin.

When I left the church the evening before, Radu and Szabina announced that training would continue the next day. I had eaten a dinner of mamaliga—a sort of porridge—and leftover vegetable stew in Szabina's home with Abe and Seward, before Elisabeta led us to our quarters for the night. Abe and Seward stayed in one of the homes with Gabriel and two other male villagers while I stayed in Elisabeta's home. She insisted that as the guest, I use the bedroom and waved away my protests as she left to sleep in the main room.

Despite my turbulent emotions, I managed to fall asleep quickly, with Jonathan's photo clutched in my hand.

As I ate breakfast with the others the next morning, Radu informed us that the scouts had returned and it was time to continue preparing for the next day's attack. He detailed the plan of penetrating the fortress, emphasizing my role as the first to approach. Multiple stunned gazes fell on me at the announcement, and I had to force myself to maintain a stoic countenance. Since I was so integral to the initial attack, Radu insisted that I train on my own and separately from the others.

I had now spent hours under Szabina's tutelage, who trained me with several other vampires from the village. I had felt Anara's eyes on me that morning, her expression indiscernible, but to my relief, I overheard Radu inform her that she was not to be included in my training after her actions the day before.

With Szabina and the others, I had practiced my flight on foot and on horseback, as well as warding off attacking vampires with my kukri, the stakes, and the wolfsbane. But I still felt desperately unprepared, and tears of frustration welled in my eyes as I dusted myself off.

"You do not have to do this," Szabina said, assessing my distress. "We can find another way to enter the—'"

"No," I cut her off, wiping at my eyes. As terrified as I was, I knew that using me as bait was the best way to weaken their initial defense. "I can do it."

"Then we need to keep training," Szabina said. "There is no time for rest."

She had barely completed the sentence when I was once again thrown back against a nearby tree, unable to move. She had placed me into a thrall. She crept towards me, her fangs bared and her eyes lethal, while the other hovering vampires watched in silence.

Though I knew Szabina would not harm me the way Anara had, fear stirred in me as the paralysis took hold. I concentrated on her eyes, as I had with Anara. And once again, I saw a flurry of images. It was like being an active part of a waking dream.

I was a young woman, encircled in the arms of a handsome male vampire. We were standing in a darkened forest clearing, and I felt a combination of both love and sorrow as his head dipped towards my throat, his fangs sinking into the soft flesh.

I was released from the hold, throwing out my arms to break my fall as I plummeted to the ground. Szabina stumbled back from me, her trembling hands pressed to the sides of her head. I took advantage of her disorientation to leap to my feet, my kukri outstretched, placing the blade against her neck as I evenly met her eyes. Szabina still looked out of sorts, but she gave me a small nod of approval.

"Nikolaus, Kudret," she said, turning towards two of the hovering vampires. I recognized them as the vampires Radu had sent on the scout to the fortress. Though one was light and the other dark—Nikolaus with light brown hair and blue eyes, Kudret with dark hair and brown eyes—they could have almost been brothers, with their similar muscular builds and striking handsome features. "Please continue her training. I–I will return."

"I would like to help," Gabriel said quietly.

I whirled in surprise as Gabriel stepped from the cluster of trees behind us. He had not said a word to me since our row in the church yesterday, and his face was conciliatory as he approached.

"If . . . if it's not a bother," he added.

"No," I said, giving him a small smile. "Not at all."

Szabina gave him a nod as she left, and we remained in the clearing until the sun began its descent towards the horizon. Gabriel and the others trained me on how to evade attacks, practice offensive moves, and even how to disguise my scent with dirt. By the time Szabina returned to the clearing to end the training, my limbs were sore and screaming with protest.

"You have done well, Mina," Szabina said as the other vampires began to file out of the clearing. "Sleep well tonight. You need to rest."

I watched her file out of the clearing after the others, wondering about the images I had seen. Who was that male vampire? What was her connection to him?

"Mina," Gabriel said, coming to stand at my side. "I want to apologize for—"

"There is no need," I said, shaking my head. "You promised our mother you would keep me safe. I understand your concern."

"It is not just my promise to her. You are my only family. I worry for you as my sister. I will not try to dissuade you again, but please be careful tomorrow. Vlad, Ilona and his followers are vicious."

"I know," I said, though a chill swept through me at his words. "I'll be careful. I promise."

"Mother said you would be headstrong. I underestimated how much," Gabriel said, his lips twitching with a wry smile as we headed back towards the village. "She said you weren't like other little girls—you had an insatiable curiosity, an intelligence beyond your years. She seemed to know you would not have a common life."

"Gabriel?" I asked, stopping as we reached the front gate of the village. He looked down at me with a raised brow. "How . . . how was she?"

I had been meaning to ask Gabriel about my mother, but my previous fear of him and shock at his very existence had prevented me from doing so. Even with all that Szabina had told me, I was still hungry for any knowledge about her.

"Kind. Loving. She had great humor. I remember once when I was still a boy, she came to the house to take me into town. She bought me a sweet ice and found a group of children for me to play street football with. I wasn't often around other children. They didn't seem to care that I looked different, and it was the most fun I'd had in quite some time. I won the first round, and when I looked over to see if Mother saw . . . there were tears in her eyes. I thought I'd done something to upset her. But when I asked her what was the matter, she assured me she was all right," Gabriel said, looking haunted by the memory. "There were many times when she was like that. Distant. Sad. I still wonder what she was thinking about when she seemed to lose herself."

His voice trailed off on the last word, and he turned from me to enter the gate, his body taut with renewed grief. As I watched him go, a powerful thought swept through my mind. *I will avenge her for you. I will avenge her for us both.*

During dinner in Szabina's home, I ate in tense silence with Abe, Seward, and Gabriel. I had no doubt they were as nervous about the next day's attack as I was. Radu stepped in to urge us to get as much rest as possible; we would be awoken to leave when it was still dark. Before he left, his gaze found mine and held it, as if searching for any hesitation, but I steadily returned his look.

When we were alone, Seward solemnly lifted his cup of water, looking at each one of us.

"A drink," he said. "To killing vampires. Ah, I mean—" he faltered, his eyes straying to Gabriel, his cheeks filling with color.

"It is no bother," Gabriel said, amused.

"To defeating *evil* vampires," Abe corrected, giving Seward a rueful smile.

We lifted our cups to meet his own. As everyone drank, I set mine down.

"I wanted to thank you all," I said. "For taking this journey with me. I was mad to think I could do this on my own."

"You and I started this journey together, before we were even aware," Abe replied. "Years ago, in that forest where your father was murdered. It is apropos that we shall finish it together."

"Let's pray we can kill those bloody things," Seward said. "God help us if we fail."

We headed to our quarters, Abe lingering behind to fall into step beside me as Seward and Gabriel went ahead.

"Are you well enough to fight tomorrow?" I asked, my eyes flickering down to his side with concern.

"Yes. I was quite all right during the training, the wound has healed well and I no longer feel any pain. You fret too much, Mina," Abe replied, giving me a wry look. "I should be the one worried about you."

"I'll be all right," I said hastily, looking up at the night sky that was blanketed with stars. I stopped walking, taking it in as a sudden memory assailed me.

"Remember the night rides we took with Father?" I asked. "To try and locate what specimens we could find in the dark?"

"Yes," he replied, with a fleeting smile.

"The stars on those nights in the countryside, it was such a beautiful sight," I mused, feeling an ache at the memory. We had not yet heard rumors of wolf attacks in the Transylvanian countryside, the tales of *strigoi* had seemed like superstitious nonsense, and the future was still rife with wonder and possibility. I had no idea of the monsters in our midst—the monsters I would be forced to confront.

"Many could die tomorrow, Mina," Abe said bluntly. His words sent me careening back to the present, and I whirled to face him, taken aback by his grim words. "I could die."

"No, Abe," I whispered. "Do not say such things. We have a plan. It will mitigate loss of life. You are certainly not going to die tomorrow. I won't hear of it."

"This whole journey we have been perilously close to death—Arthur's demise proves it. Tomorrow we will be closer to it than we ever have before. If I do die tomorrow," he continued gravely, taking a step closer to me, his voice dropping to an intimate whisper. "Rescue your fiancé. Take him home to London, marry him, and live the life your mother wanted you to live. Away from monsters and darkness. Live in the light of the sun. After all that you have been through, I want you to be happy, Mina. Your happiness is all that I have ever wanted."

I could tell there was something he wasn't telling me, something that he dare not say aloud, and I suspected I knew what it was. He was studying me intently, waiting for my response—

needing my promise, as Arthur had on that boat in the North Sea.

But I would not give him the promise he wanted to hear. His words stirred up dormant emotions that once again rose to the surface, only this time I did not try to suppress them. I had realized something I long suspected to be true; something I'd tried to deny for three long years. Though I loved Jonathan with all of my heart, I also loved Abe, and I could not bear the thought of losing either of them. I would ride to the ends of the earth to rescue him, just as I had with Jonathan.

"I can't promise you that," I said, my eyes locking with his. He paled at my response, and I continued. "Yes, I will rescue Jonathan and take him home. But if you die tomorrow... I will never be happy again. You stay alive, Abraham Van Helsing."

6

FORTRESS OF BLOOD

The fortress was perched on a low peak of the Carpathians, the spires of its towers winding out of the fog and towards the early morning sky like a fallen angel beseeching the heavens. My hands quivered as I gripped the reins of my horse, guiding it up the precariously steep mountain path that led to the fortress' gatehouse. I could almost feel the hesitation in the tightly coiled muscles of my horse as he clamored up the path; it was as if he somehow knew we were entering the realm of monsters.

I cast a glance back down the mountain path, towards the cluster of trees at the base where Radu, Szabina, Anara, Gabriel and the others were lying in wait.

Before we had left the fortified village, hours earlier when night still warded off the dawn, Radu had briefly ran through the plan once more.

Human volunteers would willingly let Vlad's scouts capture them, whom Nikolaus and Kudret had witnessed patrolling the outskirts of the fortress. Abe, Seward, Elisabeta, and several of the human villagers had bravely volunteered for the task. Soon after their capture, I would approach the fortress on my horse, making sure to be in full view of the watchtowers. When the gatehouse doors lifted and Vlad's vampires inevitably came towards me, I was to turn around and ride back down the path and into the surrounding forest, where Radu and the other vampires would be waiting. Together, they would surround the attacking force and slaughter them, and we would all enter the fortress through the open gates.

Abe, Seward and the other human volunteers had left ahead of us, their clothes dirty and torn, disguised as roaming peasants. Seward had given me a warm embrace of farewell, but Abe had tactfully avoided me, not even meeting my eyes as he climbed onto his horse. When I'd hurried forward to bid him farewell, his eyes only briefly met mine and he'd given me a curt nod before he galloped away. I watched him go with a searing aguish in my chest, silently praying that I would see him again. But I had set it aside, forcing myself to focus on the battle that lay ahead as I made my way out of the village and towards the fortress.

Our journey had been silent with foreboding. The forests had seemed to deepen and grow thicker as we drew closer to the fortress, and it truly felt as if we were leaving civilization behind and entering a dark world where nightmares were a reality.

We finally arrived at the base of the fortress as the sun began its ascent into the sky, hiding ourselves in a cluster of trees. Gabriel had dismounted and, without a word, pulled me into his arms. Though his skin bore the cold of a vampire, I felt a surprising warmth at his touch, and I leaned into his embrace. When he stepped back, his face was shadowed with worry. I suspected there was much more he wanted to say, but his words were brief.

"Be safe, sister," he whispered.

Radu and Szabina gave me assuring nods, while Anara met my eyes with a look of detached impassiveness. I mounted my horse, leading him on a slow trot out of the forest and up the mountain path.

Now, as I made my way closer to the fortress, I could see the barbican leading towards the imposing iron gatehouse, and my pulse increased, battering away at my skin. I had no doubt that I had been seen from one of the towers, and it was only a matter of time before I was pursued. I brushed my fingers against the kukri that was tucked beneath the left sleeve of my dress, and the second one that was tucked beneath my right sleeve. There was a stake and a knife stowed in my bodice, along with a pouch of wolfsbane, which was also wound into my tight bun.

Despite my weapons, I felt great trepidation at the thought of what I would soon face, and my hands trembled even more as I gripped the reins. I forced myself to think of Jonathan, trapped somewhere inside the imposing fortress, and the thought was all I needed to urge my horse forward until we were moving in a full gallop towards the gatehouse.

Up ahead, the jagged iron gates of the fortress slowly screeched upwards, but no one came out. I pulled back on the reins of my horse, bringing him to a complete stop, and scanned the courtyard that lay behind the gates. Thick fog encased the courtyard, and after several long moments that seemed suspended in time, a small group of figures emerged like apparitions through the fog.

Vampires clamored out of the gatehouse and down the path of the barbican, their fangs bared in fierce snarls.

I recognized one of them. It was Matyas, the vampire in Budapest who had refused to join us. Rage and panic flared in my chest at the sight of him. If he was on Vlad's side, he must have told him of our plan.

I acted quickly, steering my horse around and clamoring back down the steep incline. The vampires' horses were getting closer, and I could almost feel the hatred radiating from the vampires as they raced after me. I kept my focus on the path downhill, my heart in my throat as I leaned forward to kick the sides of my horse, urging him to gallop even faster.

But soon one of the vampire's horses closed in on me, until we were parallel. Panic coursed through me, but I kept my gaze straight ahead. I reached for the knife tucked in my bodice, but a strong arm snaked around my waist from the side, yanking me from my horse and tossing the knife from my hand.

I screamed, struggling in my captor's arms as my horse continued to clamor down the mountain. I twisted my head around to see Matyas' icy eyes, his grip tightening around my waist. The wolfsbane tucked in my dress and wound throughout my hair clearly had no effect on him, as he reached into my bodice and my hair to toss it aside while I fruitlessly struggled to release myself from his viselike grip. He steered his horse back towards the fortress, the other vampires continuing their progress down the mountain, and I realized with horror that they must know that others were waiting.

Beneath my fear, a wave of overwhelming despair swelled. I had failed before our plan had a chance to unfold, and my failure would lead to even more deaths. I could not stifle the strangled sob that escaped my throat, making one last desperate attempt to yank free of Matyas' grip.

"Keep struggling and your death will not be quick," he hissed, his lips cold against my ear. "I can keep you alive for days . . . as we did your mother."

I froze in shock, my eyes filling with horrified tears. Had Matyas been one of the vampires who had tortured and killed my mother? I recalled the brief flare of recognition in his eyes when he saw me in Budapest, and rage seized me.

"Why are you doing this?" I asked, forcing myself to speak through a maelstrom of panic and fury. I needed to push past my unstable emotions and focus. I still had my kukri knives and the stake; I prayed that he did not find and remove them. There was still a chance of getting away, but I needed to keep him distracted. "Radu trusted you."

"Radu is a fool. He refuses to see what is certain to come," Matyas spat. "As are you. We are too powerful and too great to be defeated—as your ancestors learned."

His grip remained firm as his horse clamored the remaining way up the mountain path and through the gatehouse.

The fog had dissipated, and I could see that the inner courtyard, which may have been stunning centuries ago, was now in a state of decay. The stone paving on the ground was cracked and disintegrating; the central gardens had grown wild with long-dead plants. The keep and surrounding buildings consisted of decaying grey stones; their windows grimy with both dust and age. The entire castle seemed heavy with the feel and stench of death.

A terrified young man stepped forward to take the horse when we clattered into the courtyard, keeping his gaze lowered out of either respect or terror, though I suspected it was the latter. Matyas leapt off the horse, taking me with him as he forcefully dragged me towards the keep by my neck, his grip bruising and firm. I managed to keep my arms close against my sides, praying that neither of my weapons would slip out.

Scores of vampires crept out of the surrounding buildings as Matyas dragged me through the courtyard, like vultures gathering around dying prey. Many of them had the same look of the ferals we had encountered, with unnatural red or black eyes and empty stares; others looked eerily human, the only telltale sign of vampirism their pale, colorless skin or their lips flushed with blood. They all trained their cold gazes on me as Matyas continued to drag me forward, and I heard some hiss *Ghyslaine* as we went by. They could easily tear me apart, and I could tell by the hunger in their eyes that they longed to. Matyas' grip on me seemed to signal to them that I was forbidden. For now.

We arrived at the entrance of the keep and the doors were swung open from the inside by another human, this one a frail woman who also kept her eyes lowered, and I could see that she was practically quaking with trepidation.

I looked around as Matyas yanked me inside. We were in a massive central foyer that had the same sense of decay as the exterior. The four winding staircases that led to the upper floors and towers were crumbling, the stone walls decrepit with age and neglect. He led me through another set of doors, opened by another trembling woman, and we were now in what must have once been a great hall, with intricate stained glass windows, ornate high vaulted ceilings, and a long wooden table in the center that nearly spanned the entire hall.

I barely noticed the decor of the room as Matyas tossed me to the floor. I fell to my knees, my loosened hair falling over my face, barely managing to keep my weapons from sliding out of my sleeves. I hastily shoved my hair out of my eyes, going still when I saw who stood before me.

It was the tall dark man and the beautiful golden-haired woman I recognized from the Langham, who I now knew were Vlad and Ilona. Standing next to Ilona, her arm wrapped proprietarily around his waist . . . was Jonathan. My Jonathan.

He looked both familiar and strange. He still wore the fine shirt and trousers he had worn to the ball. But he was now pale, his lips colorless, the usually warm hazel eyes foggy and unfocused. He was thinner, and barely seemed able to hold himself upright, leaning heavily on Ilona for support. But most disconcertingly, he studied me without a trace of recognition, only a mild curiosity.

Oh God, I thought in a panic. *What have they done to you?*

"Jonathan," I whispered, focusing only on him and not the monsters who surrounded him. "Jonathan, it's me, Mina. Are you all—"

"He is no longer your love," Ilona hissed, her brilliant green eyes glittering with fury. Her voice was light and melodious, and even tinged with rage it possessed an air of seduction. "It was foolish for you to come here, Wilhelmina."

"Matyas tells me you intend to destroy us," Vlad said, his cold dark eyes trained on me, as Matyas stepped forward to join them. His voice was older than his appearance, oddly hypnotic and rich, filling the large hall with its volume, and I recognized it from Westminster Bridge. His was a voice and a presence that was used to command. "But you and the Order are far too late to stop us. My loyal followers all over Europe are ready to strike. We will soon be at our rightful place in the world."

An ominous chill crept through me as I recalled Abe's fateful words in London. *Strange murders all over Europe*, he had said. *Berlin. Paris.*

Amsterdam. Was Vlad right? Were we too late? Would Europe inevitably fall to these monsters?

Once again, I forced myself to focus. I carefully angled my arm so that the hilt of one of my kukri knives rested at the base of my palm. One quick and well-aimed throw and I could lodge it into Vlad's heart; but the others would instantly be on me, and I would be dead.

Where were the others? Had Abe and the human villagers been found out? Had the group of vampires with Matyas already slaughtered Radu and the others? If I was truly on my own, I had no chance of escape.

"Why did you come here?" Ilona demanded. "Jonathan is lost to you now. He will soon be one of us. Humans have had their time. It is time for a new world."

"You're mad," I whispered, trying not to panic at her words about Jonathan, as I subtly dislodged the kukri from my sleeve. If I could move quickly enough, perhaps I could distract them by injuring Vlad before grabbing Jonathan. It was a large fortress with plenty of places to hide until the others—if they were still alive—came to my defense. "Humans outnumber your kind," I continued, gripping the hilt in my hand. "You all will be killed en masse if you even attempt to—"

"Your mother spoke similar words," Matyas interjected with a cold sneer. "Do you know how she died? Screaming in agony."

"As did your father," Vlad added, infuriatingly casual. "How appropriate that their meddling daughter will die in the same manner."

Rage flooded through my entire body, only this time I made no effort to quell it. My hand was on the hilt of my kukri as I leapt to my feet, swinging it out in an arc towards Vlad. Vlad caught the blade in his hand with ease, his palm going crimson with blood as he clutched it, tossing it to the ground.

And I was instantly airborne, hurled back against the far wall and paralyzed as he put me into a thrall. In a movement so fast that I could not track it with my naked eye, he was instantly before me, his black eyes burning as he wrapped one large hand around my throat and began to squeeze.

7

ESCAPE

Vlad's eyes were shut as his hands squeezed the air from my throat. I was unable to release myself from the thrall. I weakly raised my eyes to meet Jonathan's disoriented ones across the room, hoping to somehow reach him, to penetrate the fog. I thought I glimpsed a small flicker of recognition in his eyes, but soon his face was gone as my vision began to dim, and I knew that I was only seconds away from losing consciousness.

I have failed you, Jonathan. I am so sorry, I thought, as the world around me began to fade.

But I was abruptly released, sliding to the cold floor, coughing and grasping at my throat as I took in great gulps of air.

My vision cleared and I looked up to see that Radu, Szabina, Gabriel, and the others had charged into the great hall, with Vlad's followers right on their heels.

Radu had been the one to release me from Vlad's grip, and his hand was now wound around his son's throat as he lifted him bodily into the air, his eyes filled with hot fury.

"This ends today, Alexandru," he roared, hurling his son over the massive wooden table to the far wall with a force so great that it cracked upon his impact.

Radu leapt across the table, temporarily airborne before landing opposite his son, who had stumbled weakly to his feet, and they began to fight in a flurry of impossibly fast moves.

Szabina raced toward Matyas, who had backed up fearfully upon their entrance. She looked more terrifying than I had ever seen her; her eyes wild, her fangs exposed.

"Traitor!" she screamed, tackling Matyas to the floor.

The great hall descended into chaos as Vlad's followers and our vampire allies began to fight; tearing into each other's flesh with their hands and fangs, snapping necks, hurling bodies across the room; their movements as rapid as a hummingbird's wings.

In the melee, I temporarily lost track of Ilona and Jonathan as I stumbled to my feet, still gasping for air. But I soon found them. Ilona was dragging the still dazed Jonathan out of the rear exit of the hall. Gabriel rushed to my side, helping me the rest of the way up as he placed my kukri in my hands.

"I'm all right," I said quickly, my eyes still trained on the rear doors, where Ilona and Jonathan had disappeared. "I'm going after Jonathan and Ilona. They've done something to him."

Gabriel nodded, gripping my arm to lead me out of the hall, but I stopped him.

"Matyas," I said, biting out the name with fury. I gestured to the center of the hall, where Szabina and Matyas stood fighting on top of the table. "He killed our mother."

Gabriel's silver eyes darkened with rage at my words, his grip going slack on my arm.

"I have my weapons. You can find me," I said, moving away from him. I could see Gabriel's hesitation, torn between his need to protect me, and his desire to avenge our mother. His rage seemed to win the battle, and he gave me an affirming nod before charging towards Szabina and Matyas.

I tore around the table and towards the exit, but a towering, wild-eyed male vampire I recognized as one of the vampires from the courtyard suddenly appeared before me and grabbed me by my neck, slamming me backwards against the table. My body reeled in agony at the painful impact, and the vampire leaned down, his fangs exposed, sinking them into my throat. I cried out at the sharp searing pain of his teeth in my flesh but managed to arch backwards, using my free hand to lodge my kukri into his back. He snarled with pain, removing his teeth from my neck as he did so, and I used the opportunity to kick him off of me as I sank my kukri into his heart. He sank to the floor, his cold hands over mine in a futile attempt to release my blade, but I held firm, even as his dark red blood flowed over my hands and his eyes fluttered shut.

I yanked out my blade and pushed past the blur of fighting bodies as I continued heading towards the door. Another vampire grabbed me from behind, but this time I managed to whirl out of her grip, continuing my desperate flight towards the door.

A hulking male vampire seemed to sense my intent and moved to stand in front of the door, his red eyes trained on mine in open challenge. My urgency to get to Jonathan was so great that I felt no fear as I charged towards him, only resolve, and when the vampire charged towards me with a snarl, I was ready.

My stake was already out, and as soon as he was a breath away, I staked him clean through his heart. As he stiffened and howled in pain, I arched my kukri towards his throat, slicing his head clear from his body, his crimson blood splattering across my face and my dress.

I kept moving, darting over his headless body towards the door, racing into the corridor just outside the hall.

The corridor was empty, and I allowed myself a moment to clutch the wall and take several deep breaths, wiping the slick blood off of my face with trembling hands. When I looked up, I caught a brief glimpse of Ilona and Jonathan's retreating forms as she dragged him up a winding staircase at the far end of the corridor.

I tore after them. When I reached the base of the staircase, I glanced up. The stairs seemed to twist and wind upwards indefinitely, leading to the apex of one of the towers, and I could hear their footsteps as they ascended.

Hiking up my skirt, I charged up the stairs. But when I reached the second curve, I was hurled against the crumbling stone wall of the tower, paralyzed.

A group of ferals scrambled towards me from the base of the stairs, their eyes blazing with eagerness and hunger as they approached. Near hysteria filled me at the sight of them, and I struggled to remain calm, searching the group for the vampire who held the thrall. My gaze landed on a stocky male vampire with a shock of ash blonde hair. He was in the very front of the group and appeared to lead the rest. His black eyes were trained on mine, his lips curled back in a snarl.

I stood in the center of a village that had been burned to the ground. Despair swept over me as I sank to my knees and wept. I felt a cold presence approach, and looked up to see a dark figure approach, opening its mouth to reveal a sharp pair of fangs.

I was released from the hold as the vampire stumbled back, looking dazed and disoriented; but the other vampires continued to charge towards me.

I turned to continue racing up the stairs, but they were close on my heels, and a feral launched herself at me from behind, tackling me down to one of the steps. She yanked my head back and I screamed as she slurped eagerly at my still bleeding neck wound, her rail-thin arms keeping me pinned to the steps with inhuman strength. My stake and kukri had slipped from my grip, and I could only watch helplessly as the other ferals surrounded us on the narrow staircase, eagerly awaiting their turn to feast.

"*Hakeel ishta mi,*" a voice hissed from further down the stairs.

The feral stiffened and instantly lifted her bloodstained fangs from my throat, turning towards the source of the voice. The ferals who surrounded us followed her gaze.

I looked down the stairs. I was startled to see

Anara standing further down the stairs. Abe hovered behind her. She was focused on the ferals, who now stood stock still, as if they were hypnotized by her strange words.

"Mina," Abe said quietly, his eyes also trained on the ferals. I could tell that he was trying to appear calm, but his voice quavered. "Anara will distract them. Move away from them, slowly."

Anara's eyes did not shift from the vampires, and they remained as still as statues.

I cautiously sat up, reaching behind me to pick up my weapons. I gingerly got to my feet, gripping both the kukri and stake should they come out of their daze and strike, but they remained perfectly still as I crept backwards up the stairs.

Anara gave Abe a small nod, keeping her focus on the ferals, and he edged around Anara to creep up the stairs, his face white with terror as he brushed past the immobile ferals and reached my side.

We turned and continued to race up the stairs. I cast one last glance back down towards Anara and the ferals as we ran, surprised that she had saved my life and wondering how she was able to control them.

"Anara was one of the vampires who freed us and the other prisoners," Abe said, panting as we darted up the stairs. "She did that same trick on our vampire guards. When we came up from the dungeons, Gabriel pulled us aside and told us where you were. I am so very relieved that we found you."

"Ilona has Jonathan," I said, my words coming out in short gasps as we ran. I could see the top of the tower now, only fifty steps away. "I don't think he's been changed yet. But something's terribly wrong. They've done something to him."

We reached the top of the stairs where a small narrow corridor led to a chamber door at the far end. The door was partially open, and I could see the shadow of two figures inside.

I sprinted forward, Abe on my heels, clutching the hilts of my kukri and stake so tightly that it felt as if my palms would bleed. I shoved open the door, which opened onto a grand bedchamber.

Jonathan and Ilona stood just outside the chamber on a narrow balcony, dangerously close to the edge. Ilona's green eyes were alight with hatred as they landed on me, while Jonathan's gaze remained unfocused. Abe entered the chamber behind me, and Jonathan's eyes slid towards him, a dark look flickering briefly across his features.

I took a cautious step towards them, terrified of what Ilona would do next. I ached to throw my blade into her heart, but she was standing too close to Jonathan. I had to get him away from her.

"Jonathan," I said desperately, trying to keep my voice steady as I addressed him. "It's me, Mina. Your fiancée. You were abducted. I'm here to take you home."

"His home is with me!" Ilona shouted, taking another step closer to the edge of the balcony, pulling Jonathan along with her. I stilled as she turned to give Jonathan a look that was both loving and dangerous. "He is with us now."

"Jonathan," I repeated, disregarding her words as I implored him with my eyes. He still looked as if he was trying to recall my identity. If I could get him to take just one step away from her, I would have a clear shot. "Please, Jonathan, I need you to remember that—"

"Jonathan," Ilona interjected, leaning seductively close to Jonathan, brushing his ear with her lips. "Kill her. Tear out her and her lover's throat."

I watched in horrified astonishment as Jonathan seemed to heed her words and immediately moved towards us. The uncertainty had vanished, and those eyes that once shone with so much love for me, were now dark with deadly purpose. From behind him, Ilona smiled.

"Jonathan!" I shouted, blinking back tears of disbelief as Jonathan stalked towards us. "Jonathan, it's me! Mina! Your Mina!"

"Mina." Abe was at my side now, his breath close to my ear, his voice panicked. "Leave now. Let me try to reach him."

"No," I said fiercely. If anyone could reach Jonathan, it was me.

I boldly crossed the chamber to meet him as he approached. Jonathan halted, another flash of confusion flickering across his face as I moved towards him. It was a moment that I seized, closing the remaining distance between us to place my hands on his face, which was dangerously feverish and clammy.

"The carriage ride down Piccadilly in London," I whispered, holding his disconcerted eyes. I prayed that this memory would pull him out of this trance and back to me. I could feel both Ilona's cold look and Abe's fearful presence, but I focused only on Jonathan. "It was raining, quite fiercely. You turned to look at me and there was so much love in your eyes. Do you remember what you said, my love? Do you remember what you asked me?"

"Jonathan!" Ilona shouted, her fury barely contained. "I gave you an order!"

"You asked me to marry you," I continued, desperate. Jonathan had stiffened at her words, and I feared that I had mere seconds before Ilona killed me and then Abe, herself. I removed my hand from his face, showing him my engagement ring, the rose gold band now splattered with blood. "I had been in such despair for so long. You brought me out of it. You made me feel happiness again. What did I say? What did I say, Jonathan William Harker?"

I used his full name in the hope that it would ignite his memory, but his eyes remained foggy and distant. Tears blurred my vision, and something broke inside of me. I felt a cold numbness as I dropped my hands to my sides, taking a step back from him.

I was too late. I had lost someone else I loved to these monsters.

"Now, *lubirea mea*," Ilona said, and I could hear the smile in her voice—the blaze of triumph. "Kill her now."

As Jonathan's hands lifted towards me, I realized that I had no fight left in me. I simply closed my eyes.

"NO!" Abe shouted from behind me. Yet he did not move, and I realized that Ilona must have put him into a thrall.

But when Jonathan's hands came to rest at the base of my throat, they were gentle. They slid up to cup my face, and my eyes flew open in surprise, rising to meet his.

It was like watching storm clouds lift to reveal the brilliance of the sun. The fog was gone, and the clear hazel eyes that peered down at me were those of the Jonathan I knew.

"You said yes," Jonathan's voice was strangled and weak, but it was his voice, the one I remembered and loved. My heart leapt in my chest with joy. "*Mina*. Oh God, Mina," he whispered tremulously.

The coldness disappeared, and my hands flew up to grasp his.

"I've come for you," I whispered, smiling through my tears. "I've come to take you home."

"Jonathan!" Ilona's voice shot out with the force of a cannon, her smug melodiousness gone. Jonathan stiffened and whirled to face her, remaining protectively in front of me as she moved away from the balcony and into the chamber.

"Have you forgotten what I showed you? What you saw in your own mind? She has betrayed you! She has brought her lover with her to kill you. Do not let her betray you once more!"

Jonathan's eyes locked with hers, and once again, I saw a haze of uncertainty and disorientation descend. I had to get him out of here, away from her.

As I stepped past Jonathan to charge towards her, I was flung back against the wall next to Abe, paralyzed. Ilona was on me at once, both her hands on the sides of my head, on the verge of snapping my neck. But she was abruptly hurled off of me, flying through the air to land on the opposite side of the chamber. Abe and I were immediately released from our paralysis, looking up in astonishment as we crumpled to the floor.

Jonathan had thrown her off of me. He now stood opposite us, looking down at his hands as he took in deep ragged breaths, amazed by his own strength.

Across the chamber, Ilona looked stunned as well, but I did not give her a change to gather her bearings. I shot to my feet, hurling my wooden stake directly at her heart. She dodged, and it landed in the side of her neck instead, followed by Abe's knife in the center of her chest, mere inches from her heart.

The blows were not fatal, but dark crimson blood seeped from her wounds, and she grimaced in pain, her face paling even more as she yanked out the stake and knife from the bleeding wounds.

Abe and I dashed towards her, my kukri already angled to slice off her head, Abe's knife outstretched to sink into her heart, but she stumbled to her feet and towards the balcony, leaping off the edge before we could reach her.

Abe and I raced to the balcony, peering over the edge. The crevasse below was a sheer drop, leading to a rocky embankment. There was no sign of her below. She'd vanished.

"Mina."

I whirled. Jonathan stood in the center of the bedchamber, still pale and shaken, but looking more like himself. His expression was haunted, as if he had just awoken from a terrible nightmare.

I hurried towards him, and his arms went around me as he buried his face in my hair, his thin shoulders trembling with sobs.

"Oh God, Mina. I thought I was dead. She did something to my mind. I could not see what was real and what was false. It was as if I was trapped in my own mind," Jonathan whispered brokenly.

"It's all right," I said, holding him as I fought back my own tears. "You are safe now. You have my word."

"Mina, Jonathan," Abe's voice came from behind us, and we turned.

Abe hovered by the doorway, his face grave. "As long as we are in this fortress, we are still in danger. We need to leave."

"Stay behind me," I said to Jonathan, gripping his hand in mine. He nodded, and we made our way out of the bedchamber.

Abe stayed several paces ahead of us as we hurried down the corridor and back down the winding stairs. Anara was still waiting further down the stairs, a group of ferals now dead at her feet.

"More tried to attack. I held them off," she said calmly. Her eyes briefly strayed to Jonathan, and I was surprised to see that there was a flicker of relief in her eyes at the sight of him. "Get to the postern gate. Radu and the others are still fighting Vlad and his creatures in the great hall and the courtyard. You must leave while they are still distracted."

She flanked us as we continued down the stairs. Once we reached the base, I could hear the furor of rapid movement as the vampires continued to fight in the great hall.

"Keep moving!" Anara hissed, gesturing towards the far end of the corridor, where I could see a stream of human prisoners hurriedly making their way towards the rear postern gate.

I clutched Jonathan's hand as we obliged her, hurrying down the corridor to join the stream of dazed and terrified humans as they fled out the gate.

I spotted Gabriel, Seward, Nikolaus, and Kudret standing at the doorway of the gate, directing the released prisoners out of the fortress. When Gabriel's eyes met mine, they softened with relief. His eyes drifted to Jonathan, and he gave me a wide smile.

At our side, Abe gestured for Seward to join us. Seward looked weak. His shoulder was bleeding and he moved with a slight limp, but his face was flushed with abject relief as he joined us, turning to take Jonathan in. He met my eyes and gave me the same congratulatory smile that Gabriel had given me, and I grinned in return.

We stepped out of the fortress and into a glaringly bright and sunny day, a stark contrast to the dreary darkness of the fortress' interior. We made our way down the rugged mountain path that led out of the gates and away from the fortress, down towards a thick patch of forest.

An almost religious silence had fallen over everyone. The prisoners around us looked as if they were still uncertain that their escape was even real. I slowly took them in. There was a young girl, no more than twelve, who moved in a shuffling gait, her arms wrapped securely around herself, her eyes bloodshot with tears. Close to her, a man of about twenty had the look of someone who had once been muscular and robust, but was now thin and frail, his skin pulled taut over his bones, his eyes dark and haunted. Right next to us, there was a trembling woman whose face was partially deformed, the skin of her right cheek torn and jagged in a crisscross pattern, and there were two open and bleeding wounds in her neck. *What horrors had these prisoners suffered?* I wondered with a shiver.

I moved closer to Jonathan, my hand steady in his. Whatever horrors they had suffered was over now, and I felt something I had not allowed myself to feel in quite some time. Hope. We would soon be far from this fortress and its evils. Radu would kill Vlad, and hopefully Ilona had not survived her fall. Their evil would die with them. The nightmare could soon be over.

My hope dimmed as I looked around. Why weren't we being stopped? Vlad had scores of vampires at his command. Were they all fighting Radu and the others, or were they lying in wait somewhere?

Instinctively, I clutched Jonathan's hand and picked up my pace, wanting to put as much distance between us and the fortress as quickly as possible. But the survivors around us moved at a lethargic pace, still reeling and disoriented from the horrors they had suffered.

As we descended into the dense forest that lined the base of the mountain, I began to relax. During our preparations, Radu had informed us there was an abandoned fortified village several kilometers away from the fortress. There we would all gather before continuing on to the nearby city of Debrecen, where we would meet up with Radu and the others at another one of his homes. I knew my anxiety would dissipate once we arrived safely in the fortified village.

"Something . . . something is not right," Jonathan whispered suddenly, halting in his tracks. I looked at him, fearful. "Something is near. I can feel it."

Abe and Seward stopped and turned to face us, the trepidation clear on their faces.

"What do you mean, Jonathan?" I asked, my throat dry.

Before he could reply, screams punctuated the silence. I whirled, watching in dazed horror as small packs of feral vampires lunged out from the surrounding trees, descending onto the helpless prisoners in a frenzied swarm.

Jonathan took charge, dashing ahead and dragging me along with him. Abe and Seward were close on our heels, their weapons out, ready to fight off any attacking vampires. I unearthed my kukri as well, prepared to defend us against any attacks.

But I soon realized that the ferals were not focused on the four of us; their attention was trained on the helpless humans around us. I desperately wanted to stop to help them, but when my steps faltered, Jonathan's hand tightened over mine.

"There are too many. We must keep running!"

I heeded his warning, and we continued to dash away from the carnage and further into the forest with another small group of humans, until the screams behind us faded into the distance. I searched around for Gabriel, but realized that he was still far behind us at the fortress, and I fervently prayed that he was all right.

It seemed as if we had been running for hours when I spotted the abandoned fortified village up ahead, similar in appearance to the one we had left this morning. Several of our vampire allies, who were dispersed throughout the group of fleeing humans, moved to flank us from the rear as we dashed towards the front gates of the village. They ushered us all inside, shutting the gates behind us.

Once we were inside the gates, Jonathan released my hand, stumbling away from me as he swayed on his feet. I reached out to steady him, but he began to convulse as he stumbled to his knees.

"Jonathan!" I cried, sinking down to my knees to hold him upright. "Jonathan, what—"

"Mina," he said mournfully, his voice strained and weak once more, his eyes filling with tears. "It is too late."

And with those words, he collapsed in my arms.

8

JONATHAN

Jonathan's mind was a blank haze; it seemed as if someone had reached into his skull to retrieve all of his thoughts and recollections. Yet he could still feel memories tugging persistently at the edge of his mind, demanding his attention, until they finally began to unfurl like a spool of thread.

He was a small boy, riding the Underground with his father for the first time, his small hand clasping his father's larger one.

He was a young man, seated next to his weeping mother at his father's funeral.

He was attending university, seated in the front row of his classroom, his mind buzzing with new ideas as his professor gave a lecture on ancient Greek law.

He was at a society ball, staring at a beautiful young woman who hovered on the edge of the dance *floor. He did not recognize her from the eligible women he had been introduced to during the Season, and he found himself unable to keep his eyes off of her. Though there was a sadness in the way she held herself—eyes downcast, shoulders slightly slumped—there was also a lightness that seemed to shine from within her, an incandescence that beckoned him to her side like a siren's song.*

The woman was seated next to him in a carriage. They were riding down Piccadilly, and the rain outside poured down onto the streets with such force that some raindrops made their way into the carriage. Her golden brown eyes were shining with love as she pressed her lips to his.

"Yes," she was saying. "Yes, Jonathan. I will marry you."

Happiness like he had never known before exploded in his chest, and he enveloped her in his arms.

He was in the ballroom at the Langham. The woman was in his arms as they danced the waltz. Mina. The woman was Mina. Her presence in his arms felt like home. But he felt a tension in her, a reticence that had grown increasingly familiar. She was hiding something from him, keeping a part of herself hidden when he wanted to know all of her.

He was standing alone now, and Mina stood opposite a man on the outside balcony of the Langham. Van Helsing. She was looking at Van Helsing, pained, and the bond—the love—between them was palpable, even from where he stood. Jealous heat rose in the pit of his stomach at the sight of them.

He was having a row with Mina, turning his back on her, his jealousy too great to heed the pain in her eyes, the shimmer of her tears. And then the ball room was pitch black. A tall man and woman with pale skin and oddly sharp teeth stood in front of him. He was unable to move. From somewhere far away, he heard Mina's distant voice shouting his name.

He was in a massive carriage, with elegant decorations and plush seating, like a carriage for the nobility of some faraway country on the continent. There were several other passengers seated in the carriage as well. Two men dressed for a ball, and a younger woman in a maid's uniform, their faces pale and blank with terror. The carriage hurtled through an unfamiliar countryside, lush with forests. Wherever it was, it was not England. He wanted to speak, to cry out, but his lethargy was too great, and he succumbed once more to the dark.

When he awoke, the carriage approached a looming medieval fortress that looked as if it had been carved from the very mountaintop it perched upon, like something out of a ghost story.

He was in a large bedchamber that smelled of musk and age, lying in the center of a four poster bed, unsure of how he had gotten there. Struggling to fight off his fatigue, he tried to sit up, but a woman was suddenly at his side, gently pushing him back down.

It was the tall woman from the Langham. Her eyes were a startling vivid green, her features so fine that they could have been cut from marble. Her hair was a mass of long golden waves, which fanned over him like a breeze as she leaned down close to him. Despite his disorientation, a primal desire stirred within him.

"You smell like oak and honey," she breathed, touching the side of his face, and he flinched. Her fingers were as cold as death. "You look just like the one I lost so very long ago. You will be mine in all things. My mate. Lubirea mea."

She smiled, and he jerked away from her, his heart thudding with dread. Her teeth were not human. They were long and sharp, like a wolf's, and he forebodingly thought of the creatures of folklore ... vampires.

As soon as he had the thought, she lunged towards his throat in an impossibly fast move, piercing its delicate flesh with those unnatural teeth. He let out a cry of agony at the pain that shot through him from the bite, and a sudden presence invaded his mind. He heard her voice, though her lips were not moving.

"I am Ilona. There will soon be a new world. You will help us. You will join us."

She was in his mind. He shrank away from her, this dark beauty who could not be human. He opened his mouth to plead with her, to beg her to let him go, but darkness enveloped him.

The hours and days began to intermingle, and he soon lost track of how long he lay there. At some point a man was in the bedchamber, standing over his bed, silently watching him. It was the man from the Langham. Like Ilona, his fine features were sharp and beautiful, but the black eyes were cold. He was asking him questions. Questions about London. When he did not answer, for he could not, his throat dry and his mind foggy, the man whirled towards Ilona, who hovered behind him.

"He needs to be lucid to help us," he hissed. "I told you not to begin the transformation until he gives us the information we need!"

"There was no need to wait," Ilona replied. "He has moments of lucidity. His strength will return to him once the transformation is complete."

"That could take weeks . . . months!" the man roared, taking a threatening step towards Ilona, who did not flinch. "Get the information or I will force it from him."

From somewhere beneath his numbness, panic flared from the place where he still existed. What information did they want from him? To what end?

The man left, and he was alone with Ilona once more. She asked him about London, and he willfully remained silent, grateful that he was temporarily lucid.

"You need to tell us some things about London,

Jonathan, or Vlad will kill you. He has already killed the other men. There are many vacant lodging houses in and around London. You have handled them in the past. We need access to them. We need to know where they are. Do you remember?"

"Why?" *he croaked. It hurt to speak, and he had to force the word past his lips.*

What other men was she referring to? And then he thought dimly of the other two men in the carriage that had brought him here, and a flicker of panic went through him.

"London will be the place where our new world begins. But we need your help, lubirea mea," *Ilona said. The desperation was gone from her voice now, replaced by a seductive purr.*

Jonathan was overcome by horror and revulsion. What was she referring to? What new world? He took in her unnaturally pale skin, the sharp teeth. Vampire, he thought again. Had he gone mad?

"Tell me, love," *Ilona whispered, her cold hand once again on his face, and he shivered with revulsion.* "Then you can sleep. I know you are very tired. You need to rest to regain your strength."

Jonathan looked away from her beautiful face. He may be fading, losing himself, or even going mad, but he would not help them. This new world was not something he would help bring about.

"Never," he said, and though his voice was faint and weak, the word was firm.

A long silence fell, and Jonathan thought that she had left the room. But when he turned back to look at her, she had gotten to her feet and now stood over him. The look on her face scared him, because it was blank, though her eyes glittered with a quiet rage, and her blood red lips curled into a dangerous smile.

"Very well, my love," she said, her voice lighter and more musical than usual, like a child taunting a butterfly. *"Very well."*

That was when the pain began.

At first, the torment was relegated to his emotions. Ilona could somehow make him see things. He could see his beloved Mina, but she was with Van Helsing, their naked bodies entwined in heated passion. Hot jealousy seared the inside of his chest like acid, and he struggled to close his mind to the images, but they were all he could see. Ilona's voice was also in his mind, her words a quiet taunt.

"Your betrothed has betrayed you. She is glad you are gone. She loves this Abraham Van Helsing. You see the truth of my words."

"No," he croaked aloud, tears rising behind his closed eyelids. *"No."*

"Yes," Ilona whispered.

She was next to him now, curled into him like a lover as he drifted in and out of consciousness, stroking his face, the coldness of her hands now oddly soothing against his feverish skin. "She is with him even now. She is coming to kill you."

Jonathan pleaded with her to stop, to release his mind, but the torment continued. All of his memories of Mina were tainted, and he could only see her with Van Helsing. They were at the ball at the Langham, kissing passionately, their eyes shining with love for each other. They were in the carriage riding down Piccadilly, pledging to wed. Again and again, they were naked in each other's arms—loving, hot and rapturous. His Mina telling Van Helsing she was glad he was gone.

"Jonathan never knew me, not truly. I never loved Jonathan. Only you. How I've longed for you."

And he was alone here, in this strange place, this fortress of blood and nightmares.

When the images finally stopped, the pain turned physical. He awoke in the grimy cell of a dungeon, his wrists chained to the stone wall behind him. Ilona and Vlad stood opposite him, and in a sudden flash, Vlad was on him, his cold hands on his throat, strangling him until he was certain death was upon him. Vlad released him, allowing him to take in some air before strangling him again, continuing the cycle until Jonathan gasped and pleaded for mercy. When Vlad finally left the dungeon, and he thought his torment was at an end, Ilona was on her knees before him, yanking his neck towards her. She drank from him, her jagged teeth *painful against his skin, and he could feel his life drain from him, making him grow even weaker still. They would then leave him alone for hours—days?—and the chains around his wrists grew so tight that his skin began to chafe with blood.*

The cycle continued like a macabre dance of death. Vlad strangling him, Ilona draining him, hours of isolation.

"Tell us what we want to know, lubirea mea."

Ilona's voice lulled him out of a black sleep. He weakly lifted his head, barely managing to meet her brilliant green eyes. He did not remember why they held him here or what he had done. He just wanted the agony to end.

"I will tell you whatever you want to know," he whispered. "But please, no more . . ."

His voice broke, and he was weeping. Her arms went around him, and he found himself leaning in to her. She turned his trembling face towards hers. She kissed him, and he numbly returned it, feeling a sudden and intense craving for her. He had been cold and lonely for so long.

He was seated in an enormous library, where maps of London, Europe, and other continents dotted the walls. Ilona was at his side, helping him sit upright. Vlad stood opposite them, watching as Ilona helped him remember, probing his mind. A long time ago, she told him, he used to be a solicitor in London. She slid a map in front of him, urging him to recall specific details. With her guidance, he was able to comb through his memory, pointing out vacant row houses, homes, and estates in and around the city. He signed documents they slid towards him. Some part of himself protested as he gave them the information, but he could not recall why.

Vlad's cold expression had vanished, transforming to one of eagerness, and he looked to Jonathan like a starved and ravenous beast who had finally been given prey to feast upon.

"You did well," Ilona said, once Vlad left the room, her beautiful face lit with a wide smile. "You can rest now."

He was back in the bedchamber, drifting in and out of consciousness. He continued to crave Ilona's presence, to want her near him. He no longer fought nor flinched when she drank from him, and he eagerly accepted her wrist when she pressed it to his mouth, whispering for him to drink.

In his more lucid moments, he realized with an odd detachment that something was happening to him. He was becoming . . . something. Something better, something greater. Something more. He could no longer recall his past; who he had been before. Occasionally, there were memories of a beautiful woman with golden eyes and black hair, but he did not know who she was, and soon the images of her faded completely from his mind.

And then he was in the great hall. That same vaguely familiar woman was on her knees in front of him. She was shouting at him, her desperation plain.

"It's me, Mina."

At her words, something stirred on the edges of his mind. A memory? Of what? But Vlad had his hands on the woman's neck, squeezing, and some small part of himself protested at the sight. All at once, there were dozens of vampires in the great hall, fighting amongst themselves, and Ilona was dragging him away, and they were once again in the bedchamber where he had spent days and nights drifting in and out of consciousness.

The familiar woman was somehow in the bedchamber with them, pleading with him.

"Jonathan, it's me! Mina! Your Mina!"

But he could not remember her. His mind was enveloped in a strange fog. Ilona commanded him to kill the woman, and he felt his feet moving forward, but the woman halted him with a memory.

The rainy carriage ride in Piccadilly. He blinked, and the memories which had always been there beneath the fog slowly resurfaced, flooding his mind in a deluge.

Mina. The woman was Mina. His hands were on her soft face as she raised tear filled golden eyes to his, smiling. His beloved Mina.

But Ilona was soon on Mina, on the verge of killing her. He threw Ilona away from her, astonished at his sudden strength.

When he ran with Mina out of the fortress of

nightmares, he felt as if he had been torn asunder. There was the Jonathan Harker of London, son of William and Mary Harker, solicitor, fiancé of Mina Murray. And there was this Jonathan. The Jonathan who still craved Ilona's presence, who possessed great strength and a strange and overwhelming thirst. He struggled to hold onto the former Jonathan, to the man he had been.

Yet as they escaped from that horrible place, everything seemed different. He could smell everything, from the salt tears of the human prisoners to the coppery smell of blood on their skin and clothes. He could hear the sound of a running creek that must have been kilometers away. He could even sense Van Helsing's anxiety for Mina, along with his obvious love for her. And he could sense an amalgamation of emotions. Rage. Pain. Fear. Desperation. Desire. And the overwhelming scent of blood. A scent he recognized from Vlad and Ilona. Vampires.

They ran, and once they were in the safety of the fortified village, the overwhelming weakness he had been battling took over his body. He now knew that he had been transformed during his captivity. He was now vampire. A monster.

He sank to his knees and whispered his goodbye to Mina, his beloved, and as soon as the words slid past his lips ... there was nothing.

9

THE CEREMONY

"His human body is dying."

Gabriel's words reverberated throughout the kitchen like a cannon shot. I closed my eyes, leaning back to support myself against the rickety table behind me, unable to stifle a strangled sob. Abe and Seward were silent, but I could sense their horror from their stricken expressions. *I was too late*, I thought hollowly. *I failed.*

After Jonathan collapsed, Abe and Seward carried him into the bedroom of a nearby empty cottage. There, he drifted in and out of consciousness while whispering about the terrifying details of his imprisonment—mental and physical torture in a dungeon, a beautiful woman draining him of his blood, her words enslaving his mind—and I had to urge him to be silent, to save his strength.

Gabriel entered moments later, and I hovered

anxiously as Gabriel and Abe examined him, exchanging grave looks. Gabriel led me out of the bedroom and into the kitchen, where he delivered his pronouncement.

Now, I remained stiff with shock as Gabriel continued. "He has lost a great deal of blood. He's begun the transformation. His human body will soon die, and he will become vampire."

"No," I rasped, wildly shaking my head as I opened my eyes, now awash with tears. I had no doubt that Ilona had given Jonathan her blood. If the transformation was still affecting Jonathan, Ilona had survived her fall and was still alive. "We can still stop it. We must stop it. We . . . we can kill his maker," I added, recalling Greta's observations back in Amsterdam. "That could stop the transformation from taking hold."

"It is possible to stop it," Gabriel agreed, after a hesitant pause. "But we would have to find Ilona quickly and kill her. Otherwise, the transformation will be permanent."

"Will giving him human blood stave off the transformation?" Abe asked. "I have the equipment to perform a transfusion."

"Yes," Gabriel replied. "But not indefinitely. The only way to stop it completely is to find Ilona and kill her."

"I can give blood for the transfusion," I said, determination rising beneath my despair. But I still felt a surge of frustration as I recalled how close I had been to killing Ilona. If only I had succeeded...

"Mina, it took some time for you to get to Vlad and Ilona," Gabriel said delicately. "It could take us even more time to hunt them down again, now that they know we're looking for them."

"Then we must move quickly. Ilona supplied him with her blood," I said, shuddering at the thought. "They must be linked, as Lucy was linked to the one who transformed her. We can track her through Jonathan."

"If her brother survived the attack on the fortress, it's likely she went to join him," Seward said. "We won't know if Vlad's been killed until we meet Radu and the others in Debrecen. We need to consider where Vlad and Ilona would go."

I realized with consternation that if they had both survived, they could be anywhere in Europe by now. Anywhere in the world. If Jonathan were unable to track her, we would lose them both.

"To . . . to London."

The voice was raspy and weak, and it came from behind us. We all whirled in surprise.

Jonathan leaned heavily against the doorway of the bedroom, struggling to hold himself upright. Worried, I hurried towards him.

"You need to be lying down. You need rest," I said gently, taking his arm and guiding him back into the bedroom. He reluctantly settled back down in the small bed, but intently held my eyes.

"Vlad and Ilona would go to London. They *are* going to London," he repeated, as the others entered the bedroom. "My memory is shaky, but I do remember that they asked me a great deal about London. They made me point out vacant row houses and estates in and around the city," he added, his voice dropping with shame.

The room fell silent at his words. Abe had correctly surmised that Vlad was planning to launch his attack from London. It was an ideal location, teeming with millions unaware of the coming danger. I set my rising panic aside, placing my hands on the sides of Jonathan's feverish face.

"Let us concern ourselves with Vlad and Ilona. You've been through enough."

Jonathan's gaze strayed to the men, seeming to hold on Abe.

"Please leave us. I wish to talk to Mina alone."

The men obliged, though I felt Abe's lingering look as he turned to leave. Once we were alone, Jonathan reached up for my hands, linking his cold fingers with mine as he pressed his trembling lips to my knuckles in a kiss. I blinked back tears as I took in the pallor of his skin, the bruises on this throat. What torment had he undergone in that fortress? If only I had gotten to him sooner.

"I'm so sorry," I whispered, my voice breaking.

"You're apologizing?" Jonathan breathed, his hazel eyes meeting mine in abject disbelief. "You owe me no such thing. You put yourself in great danger to rescue me. That woman—that creature—did something to my mind. My thoughts were not my own. Had I been kept there any longer, I would have been lost forever."

He reached out to pull me into his arms, lovingly stroking my hair. We sat still in each other's arms for a long moment; the only sound in the room my ragged breaths and his faint ones. *He is here with me now*, I assured myself. I had rescued him from those monsters, and I would stop the transformation from taking hold. I had to. I blinked back more tears, tightening my grip around him, as if to prevent him from being taken once again.

"I remember being at the Langham, and then in a carriage. We were traveling through the countryside, and then I was—" he haltingly began.

"Jonathan, no. You have just been through a great ordeal. You do not have to tell me about it now," I protested, recalling his delirious whispers about his imprisonment with a shudder.

"I–I want to. I fear it is the only way to purge the memories from my mind. And it could help you," he replied.

I had to force myself to remain stoic as he told me what he recalled of his time with Vlad and Ilona. The other two male vampires who had come to the Langham with Vlad and Ilona were loyal followers of Vlad, but he never saw them while he was imprisoned in the fortress. He had lost track of the women who had also been abducted, nor did he have any contact with the other prisoners. He had been kept in a bedchamber away from anyone else. He did confirm that Vlad had killed the other two men kidnapped from the ball, and I surmised that the young maid had not survived as well—we hadn't seen her amongst any of the prisoners.

I stifled my jealousy as he told me of Ilona's attentions and her obvious desire for him. I realized that Jonathan had been abducted not only for his knowledge of vacant housing in London, but because of Ilona's apparent obsession with him, and that was likely the reason Vlad had not killed him. She wanted him as her mate.

When he was finished, he looked thoroughly unsettled. I moved closer to him, wrapping my arms around him and holding him close.

"You are safe from her now," I whispered. "I promise."

"I know that this is not an illness," he said, after a long stretch of silence. "What I saw in that fortress . . . I would not have believed if I didn't see it with my own two eyes. I–I know what is happening to me. I–I am changing. Becoming like those monsters. Vampires," he concluded with a whisper.

"No," I said fervently, pulling back to hold his stricken gaze. "I will not let that happen. I'm going to kill the creature who did this to you. It'll stop the transformation from taking hold."

"I am very weak, Mina. Even if you do kill her, I do not know how much longer I have. My mind is still not my own, and I fear I am losing myself as I become this . . . this creature. If I should die, or lose myself, what I would regret most in the world is that we were never wed."

"You will not lose yourself, and you will not die," I insisted. "Stop this talk, Jonathan. Try to rest, and we'll—"

"You must listen to me," Jonathan interrupted, his voice strained with both fatigue and urgency. "It is already happening. I was a shadow of myself. You have brought me back, but I fear it is only temporary. I feel as if my grip on sanity is slipping, and my love for you is my only anchor," he added, his eyes glistening with tears. "While I am still lucid, while I am still Jonathan Harker, my only desire is to marry you, my darling."

"And we will," I said, my uneasiness growing at the graveness of his words, the finality in his voice. "As soon as we return to England, we'll—"

"I do not know if my mind will hold that long. Will you marry me today, Mina? Here?"

His pained eyes met mine, shimmering with tears of hope and anguish. *He truly thinks he will not survive*, I thought with horror. Did he not know that I would do everything in my power to prevent that from happening? Had I not traveled across Europe to rescue him?

I opened my mouth to protest, but stopped

myself when I took in the desolation in his eyes. He had gone through great agony at the hands of those monsters. How could I deny him this? We were already pledged to wed. If I could provide him with some light, some hope, then I should do so. Ignoring the brief flare of uncertainty that flared in my chest, I leaned forward to press my lips against his.

"Yes, Jonathan," I whispered against his mouth. "I will marry you today."

AFTER JONATHAN FELL into a fitful sleep, I left the house to enter the small church in the central square, where most of the others had gathered. I pulled Gabriel, Abe and Seward aside to tell them of Jonathan's desire to wed me here in Transylvania. Abe stiffened, but remained silent, while Seward and Gabriel looked worried and confused.

"There's no time," Seward protested. "We leave early tomorrow for Debrecen—we still don't know what happened to the others. We're not even sure it's safe to stay in this village for the night."

"Jonathan is very weak," Gabriel added, frowning. "He still needs a transfusion and some recovery time afterwards. Haven't you been betrothed for some time? Why the urgency?"

"He worries he will not survive much longer. I'm unable to convince him otherwise. He has gone through such torment at the hands of those monsters. I know the timing is not practical, but I want to do this for him."

"Then you should wed," Abe spoke up, his eyes shuttered and unreadable as he stepped forward.

"I can perform the transfusion now. He can rest for the remainder of the day, and you can wed tonight."

"Thank . . . thank you," I said with hesitation, a strange heaviness pressing down on my chest at his words.

"I will begin preparations," Abe said, not meeting my eyes, as he turned to leave the church. Seward hurried after him to help, and I was left alone with Gabriel.

"I'll have the other vampires patrol the outskirts of the village," Gabriel said. "If it's not safe, or they scent ferals, we cannot stay here, Mina. The ceremony will have to be postponed."

"All right," I said reluctantly. "But I do not wish to delay the ceremony any later than Debrecen. I want to ease Jonathan's anxiety."

"Is this what *you* want, Mina?" Gabriel asked, his silver eyes probing mine. "To be wed under these circumstances?"

"What I want is those monsters and their followers destroyed," I shortly replied. "But I have failed in both those undertakings. This is the least I can do for my fiancé."

I headed back to the cottage, where Abe was preparing a now sedated Jonathan for the transfusion with Seward's help. Abe only spoke to give me instructions, and I rolled up my sleeve, holding still while he extracted blood from my veins.

"We must allow him to sleep," Abe said, getting to his feet once he had completed the transfusion. His tone was brusque, and he was still not looking at me. "We will see how he is functioning after he wakes. If all is well, you can wed tonight."

They left me alone with Jonathan, and I approached his bedside. He was in the deep throes of sleep, and I could see that the transfusion had already restored some of his color. I pressed a kiss to his forehead, tenderly brushing his sweat-dampened hair back from his face, before leaving him to his slumber.

The remainder of the day went by swiftly. I learned from Gabriel that the vampires patrolling the exterior of the village had not sensed any ferals in the forest, so it was safe for us to remain until our departure the next day. There was still no sighting of Radu and the others. Nikolaus and Kudret had bravely ventured back to the outskirts of the fortress and found it to be completely abandoned. I prayed that Radu had been successful in killing Vlad, and that we only had Ilona to focus on.

As the day wore on, I studied the other released prisoners. They were young and old, male and female. From their clothing, I could tell that most of them were villagers from the surrounding countryside, while some wore fashionable city clothing. Seward moved through the village, in full inspector mode, questioning many of them, while Abe performed cursory exams on others. A small group of older men and women sat huddled in a corner of the village, whispering amongst themselves, likely recounting their ordeal. Some still looked shaken, roaming absently around the central square, staring at nothing. Others had thrown themselves into the practical task of preparing a meal of bread and salted meats they found in storage cells along the fortress walls, and searching the long-untended gardens for edible vegetables. No matter what their state, they all seemed to be coming back to life, as if realizing that their liberation from the fortress was real, and they were truly free of the monsters who had tortured and imprisoned them.

One of the men seemed to sense my curiosity and approached to tell me his story. He had left his small village on foot to head into town to purchase food from the markets. He had heard rumors of strange happenings in the forests, but had assumed they were mere nonsense and superstition.

"Wolf attacks. No more than that, I thought," he said, bitterness edging his words. "I had a weapon—I could keep wolves away."

"What happened?" I asked. "The night you

were taken?

"I felt . . . a cold. Snow on my skin. Three men surrounded me. No, not men. Monsters. Devils. Could tell they weren't human by the looks of them. Was going to use my axe on them, but they were fast. Strong. One of them, he got me, here," he said with a shudder, and I could see the scar on his neck. "I thought—I thought I'd be dead. I came to in a dungeon. All manner of people. Women, men, even some young. The monsters gave us bread once a day to eat. Every day, they'd take someone. We'd never see 'em again. Thought they were killing 'em. Found out later they were changing 'em. Making them into monsters. With blood."

I closed my eyes with a shudder. Though it had been confirmed through my own eyes that Vlad was building an army, it was still chilling to hear the words out loud.

"If you and your friends hadn't come, none of us would've lived," the man said, his eyes meeting mine. "Thank you for what you've done."

I nodded, not meeting his eyes. He was right. No one would have survived in that fortress had we not come. But had I believed those villagers several years ago, perhaps none of this would have happened.

Jonathan awoke as evening fell and gave me a small smile, looking more like himself. Abe examined him and confirmed that he was well enough to take part in a ceremony. I embraced Jonathan and told him to get more rest, and left to approach Elisabeta, the only other human woman I was acquainted with here, who had survived the fortress attack relatively unscathed.

I explained that Jonathan and I wished to be wed here, and asked if she would be willing to help me prepare for a small wedding ceremony. I braced myself for a response of disbelief, even anger, but her eyes misted over with tears, and she pulled me into her arms in a spontaneous embrace.

"Mina," she murmured. "There been much evil. We need something happy. Weddings bring joy. I talk with others. They happy to help."

Elisabeta recruited several other women, and to my surprise, their eyes also lit up at the prospect of a nighttime wedding ceremony. I handed over my traveling bag, and they went through my few items of clothing until they settled on the best dress I had brought with me, a traveling dress of deep blue silk that would serve as my makeshift wedding gown. Elisabeta bravely ventured into the surrounding forest with a vampire escort, returning with bunches of white wildflowers that would be wound throughout my hair and serve as a bouquet. They adorned the church with various candles, and one of the women miraculously found a chaplain amongst the human survivors, who happily agreed to perform the ceremony. I was so overwhelmed at the lengths Elisabeta had gone to help me, my eyes filled with tears as I thanked her.

"You save lives of many here. Happy to help you wed your Jonathan."

She ushered me to an empty cottage, where I dressed. I opted to leave my hair down, and carefully wound the wildflowers throughout my hair. I took in my reflection in an old cracked mirror propped against the wall. I had assumed that our wedding would take place in a church in one of the more fashionable neighborhoods of London, filled with guests astonished at the fact that Jonathan was actually going through with wedding the scandalous Robert Murray's daughter, their spurious smiles shielding their disapproval.

I studied my shadowed eyes and bruised throat in the mirror. I looked more like a battle survivor than a bride. Doubt flickered through me, a feeling that went beyond my unease about the rushed circumstances in which I was getting married.

"You love Jonathan?" Elisabeta asked, entering the room behind me, her gaze sweeping over my troubled features with concern.

"Of course," I replied, sounding more cross than I intended.

"You wear dark look. Not look of bride," Elisabeta said, hesitant.

"These are hardly ideal circumstances," I said stiffly. "I want to marry him when he's well, and those creatures destroyed."

"Put dark thoughts away. My wedding the best day of my life," Elisabeta urged. "My husband, I knew him when we children. We grew up together. He my love," she whispered, her voice breaking. She closed her eyes briefly and gave me an apologetic smile. "I not talk of such things on your wedding."

"No," I said gently, reaching out to touch her hand briefly. "You can tell me about him."

She hesitated for a moment, before continuing, "There was an attack on our village. The *strigoi* came in the night. Me and my Luca ran. We were holding hands. I held onto his hand very tight. But his hand, it fell from mine. A *strigoi* leapt on me, almost tore out throat. Luca moved him off me. Told me, 'Run, Elisabeta'. I could not do it—I could not run. But he begged . . . even as that monster tore into him, he begged." Her eyes filled with a fresh wave of tears. "So, I run. I run and found place in forest to hide. When I come back, Luca—his body was—"

She dissolved into sobs and I moved forward to envelop her in my arms, overcome with a wave of sympathy.

"Elisabeta, I am so sorry," I whispered, feeling another swell of rage for the creatures who had left so much despair in their wake. "I am so very sorry."

Elisabeta's sobs subsided and she pulled back, looking embarrassed as she wiped her eyes.

"You have chance to be happy," she whispered, finally meeting my eyes. "Take it."

"I will," I promised fervently, pushing my lingering unease aside. "Thank you, Elisabeta. For all you've done."

"No thanking me," she said, stepping back. "Go. Wed your Jonathan."

When I left the cottage, I saw that the dozens of humans who had escaped with us from the fortress were now gathered around the church. They turned to face me as I stepped out of the cottage, their faces lit with smiles as I approached, and I realized that Elisabeta was right. These people had experienced so much tragedy. They needed to witness something joyous.

I returned their smiles as I moved towards the open doors of the church, where Gabriel and Seward stood waiting. I looked around, but Abe was nowhere to be seen. Gabriel gave me a tentative smile, stepping forward to extend his arm. A sudden and swift pang of longing for my father pierced me. How I wished that he were here for this moment. I set aside the longing, taking Gabriel's arm, feeling a surprising amount of gratitude for his presence. I gave Seward a brief nod, which he returned with a smile, and entered the church.

I gasped. The plain interior of the church had been transformed. It was lit by dozens of candles, giving it the appearance of a *chappelle ardente*.

The pews had even been strung with the same wildflowers I wore in my hair, and they were also scattered about the scratched wooden floors.

Jonathan stood in front of the altar next to the beaming chaplain, wearing a new black sack coat, paired with a vest and trousers that I suspected had been loaned from Seward or Gabriel. He still looked pale and slightly weak, but his smile was radiant, and his eyes shone with love. As I met his eyes, a familiar warmth spread through me. *This is the man I have chosen*, I told myself as I suppressed my fretfulness. *This is the man I'll spend my life with.*

When we reached the altar, Gabriel stepped back and Jonathan grasped my hands firmly in his. The others filed in, taking their seats in the pews and crowding the aisles, reverently silent. Jonathan and I held each other's eyes as the chaplain began the ceremony. Our vows were brief and when the chaplain declared us man and wife, Jonathan pulled me close, resting his forehead against mine.

"Mina Harker," he whispered tremulously. "My darling. My life."

He leaned down to kiss me, but froze, and abruptly jerked back from me. I watched in stunned horror as the whites of his eyes turned completely black. His hands shot out to wrap around my throat, squeezing with tremendous force, and amidst terrified screams and shouts, I slipped from consciousness.

10

A DANGEROUS IDEA

"He tried to kill her!"

Abe's furious words roused me from my sleep, and I opened my eyes. I was lying in the same bedroom where Jonathan had recovered after his collapse. The door was closed, but I could hear Abe's voice clearly from the kitchen.

"If you had not stopped him—" Abe continued, his voice rising in anger.

"He stopped himself," Gabriel interjected. "That's why he asked to be placed under guard. You saw how horrified he was at what he'd done. The transformation has altered his mind."

I groggily sat up, their words igniting my memories of what happened the night before. I was still wearing my makeshift wedding dress, and the wildflowers were still wound throughout my hair. I recalled the church decorated with candles and wildflowers, Jonathan's hazel eyes shining with love, those same eyes turning black, and . . .

My hands flew to my throat at the memory. It seemed like something out of a nightmare, but the bruising around my throat confirmed that what happened was terrifyingly real.

"We need to separate Jonathan and Mina until we kill Vlad and Ilona, but they are not to be a part of this," Abe was saying now. "We can find them safe places to hide when we return to London. The three of us and whoever else is willing to help, can then focus on killing those creatures."

I abruptly got out of bed at his words, crossing the room to yank open the door and marching out. Gabriel and Abe were facing off in the center of the small kitchen, while Seward warily leaned against the table behind them. They all turned to faced me as I entered the room.

"I heard everything. What happened last night changes nothing, Abe," I said sharply, glaring at him. "I will not stand aside while you finish the fight I started. Surely, you must know that? Where is Jonathan?"

"He's alone in another cottage, guarded by two vampires—by his own request. He fears he will try to harm you again," Gabriel said gently, taking a concerned step towards me. "Do you remember what happened?"

"Yes," I said, with great difficulty, as I recalled

Jonathan's black eyes in the chapel. "But I know it was not Jonathan who harmed me. Not truly. It's the transformation—and whatever Ilona's done to his mind. We saw the same thing in Lucy Holmwood."

"Your husband," Abe said, practically spitting the word as he advanced towards me, "did not merely harm you. He nearly strangled you to death, and barely stopped himself in time. It is not safe for you to be alone with him. If we do not get to Ilona soon—"

"We will," I interrupted sharply. "We're leaving today, are we not? Once we meet up with the others, we can take the Orient Express back to England. That will get us to London quickly. Now, I want to see Jonathan."

"Mina, Jonathan's not—" Seward began, shaking his head.

"I will arm myself and fight him if I must, but I do not think that'll be necessary. I brought him back to himself in the fortress. I can help keep his mind at ease. Isolating him is not going to help," I said, turning to head towards the door. I wasn't going to wait for their permission. "I'm going to see my husband."

Abe and Seward didn't follow or try to stop me, but Gabriel hurried after me, reluctantly leading me towards a lone cottage on the far edge of the village square, where the vampire Nikolaus stood guard. He stiffened in surprise at my approach, but after a look from Gabriel, he stepped aside.

"Take this. Please," Gabriel said, removing one of my kukri knives from his pocket and handing it to me. I hesitated, but the look in his eyes broached no argument. I grudgingly took it before we both entered the cottage.

My heart broke at the sight that greeted us. Jonathan sat on the scratched wooden floor of the barren cottage, his face buried in his hands, his shoulders drooped with misery. I turned, gesturing for Gabriel to leave us, and after a moment of hesitation, he obliged.

"Stay away from me," Jonathan said once we were alone, without looking up. "I fear I will hurt you again."

"I will do no such thing," I said, taking a tentative step towards him. "We are husband and wife now. We'll fight this together."

"I–I do not know what happened," Jonathan said brokenly, finally looking up at me with anguished eyes. "I was fully myself, and so very happy. But the images she put in my mind of you and Van Helsing . . . I kept seeing them, and my hands—"

"You must fight, Jonathan. Use that same strength you had in the fortress to hold on to your mind," I urged, taking another step forward.

He shot to his feet, backing away from me,

holding out his hands to indicate that I should come no further.

"I can sense everything now—even emotions. It is agony," he said brokenly. "I can even sense your love for him."

"Have I not traveled across Europe to save you? Does that not prove the depth of my love for you?" I demanded, feeling the growing weight of despair in my chest. "Did I not marry you last night?"

"I do not doubt your love for me," Jonathan said, with a sad smile. "But I know you love him as well. I–I suspected it that night at the ball, but I can truly sense it now. Do you deny it?"

I hesitated. I now knew that my love for Abe had never completely dissipated. Jonathan deserved my honesty.

"No," I said finally, and he blanched, but I boldly stepped forward until I was within reach of him, gripping his arms. "But our relationship has long been over. You are the one I married, Jonathan. You are the one I risked my life to save."

"I know," Jonathan whispered, turning away from me and closing his eyes. He pressed his fingers to his lids, as if he wanted to physically suppress whatever he was seeing in his mind's eye. "But I need you to stay away from me."

"Jonathan," I pleaded, tears springing to my eyes. "This is not you. We vowed just last night to—"

"I need you to stay away because I love you," he said raggedly, still not looking at me. "I am not the same man I was. I will soon be a monster. I never should have made you marry me."

"You did not make me marry you!" I cried. "We were already engaged. I wanted to marry you! Don't let what that monster has done to your mind control you. I will kill her, you will be healed, and we will live as husband and wife—as we intended before any of this happened."

"I need time," Jonathan said, after a long pause, taking another step away from me. "Until—and if—you kill Ilona, and my mind returns to me, it is best that we remain apart. And . . . and I need Van Helsing to stay away from me as well."

I stared at him in disbelief, but by the rigidity of his body and the set of his jaw, I could tell that he meant every word. I tried to move closer to him, but he took several steps back until he was against the wall, holding up his hands to impede my approach.

"Am I to be punished for having a past before you? For loving him before you?" I demanded incredulously. "We have just wed. I will not allow you to give up on us."

"You have no choice," Jonathan said, meeting my eyes with a coldness that I had never seen in him before. "This is not a punishment. It is for your safety, Mina."

He abruptly moved past me, keeping his

distance as he moved to the door to swing it open. I looked at him, pleading with my eyes, but his expression was rigid.

Furious, I stalked past him to leave the cottage. I kept walking until I found another nearby empty cottage, entering and closing the door behind me.

I slid to the floor, wrapping my arms around my body as I allowed my despair to take hold, and I began to weep.

When we departed two hours later, I had managed to compose myself, and my face was a stoic mask as I rode out of the village alongside Gabriel, Abe, and Seward. Jonathan rode ahead with Nikolaus and Kudret, not sparing me a glance, and a stab of pain pierced me at his blatant disregard.

After my row with Jonathan, Abe, Gabriel and Seward's curious gazes followed me when I returned to the cottage to change and pack my bag; but I said nothing to them. Jonathan and I were married now, and I was determined to keep our discord between us. I could only hope that he would come to his senses during the journey back to London.

We encountered nothing out of the ordinary during our short journey to Debrecen, but this made me feel unsettled. Since our violent departure from the fortress, there had been no new attacks, and I knew that Vlad had scores of followers in Transylvania. Where had they all gone?

I set aside the disturbing thought as we arrived in Debrecen. With its colorful homes, baroque style buildings and medieval cobblestoned streets, it reminded me of a smaller and more intimate version of Budapest.

We separated from the released humans once we were safely in the boundaries of the city. Some had family in Debrecen, while others were heading to Budapest and other nearby cities. Elisabeta gave me a warm embrace before departing with the others, and I urged her to be safe.

The remaining group consisted of me, Gabriel, Abe, Seward, Jonathan, and four of our vampire allies—including Nikolaus and Kudret. We continued towards the stables near Debrecen's central square, where we left our horses. Gabriel led us to Radu's nearby home, which was a near replica of the one he owned in Budapest, with a yellow stucco façade and surrounded by tall iron gates.

"Radu?" Gabriel called out as we entered, trailing him down the narrow entrance hall. "Anara?"

He was met with silence, and dread stirred in the pit of my stomach. We followed Gabriel into the drawing room, where Anara, Szabina, and five more of our vampire allies that I recognized from Szabina's village were gathered. The looks on their faces ranged from shock, to grief, to despair. Anara and Szabina were seated on two plush chairs opposite the fireplace, and they barely acknowledged us as we entered the room. My sense of dread increased when I noticed that Radu was not seated amongst them.

"Anara?" Gabriel asked, his voice quivering. "Where... where is Radu?"

When Anara looked up, I saw her eyes were filled with a sheen of blood tears. She did not need to speak for us to know of Radu's fate.

"No," Gabriel whispered.

Around me, the others gasped and let out strangled sobs of grief. Seward paled, and Abe leaned back heavily against the wall, burying his face in his hands.

Though I had only known Radu briefly, my chest became heavy with my own grief for the creature who had displayed such kindness and empathy towards us. But beneath my grief, I felt a pang of guilt. If we had never come to him in Budapest, he would still be alive.

"What happened?" I asked, dreading the answer.

"We were surrounded by Vlad's followers in the great hall," Szabina replied. "Radu saved us. He led Vlad and his followers out to the courtyard.

He knew he was the main focus. We tried to go after him, but a group of ferals attacked us."

"I almost made it to him," Anara spoke up, her voice strained, blood tears streaking down her face. "I managed to get to the courtyard, where Radu and Vlad were fighting. But before I could approach, that traitor Matyas held me down. He made me watch Radu and Vlad fight. I thought Radu would be able to overpower his son, but I underestimated how deep Vlad's hatred runs for his father. I was helpless. I could do nothing," Anara faltered, pressing her hand to her mouth. Szabina reached out to place her hand on Anara's shoulder.

At the mention of Matyas' name, Gabriel and I exchanged a dark look as we realized that the creature who had killed our mother was still alive.

"Vlad tore out Radu's throat," Szabina whispered with great difficulty. Anara buried her face in her hands, as if she were trying to block out the images of Szabina's words. "Then he ripped out his heart while it still pumped."

"The pain in my father's eyes," Anara rasped, her voice heavy with tears. "As he looked at his own son . . . dying at his hands . . . I will never forget it. I screamed. I cannot recall what happened afterwards. I know Matyas released me, and Vlad fled the fortress, taking his remaining followers with him. We buried Radu at the fortress. After this is all over, and I kill his monstrous children, I will bury him next to his Ludmila."

My own tears swelled, temporarily blurring my vision. I could tell that Radu had loved his son, even though he knew what a monster he was. What agony it must have been to die at his hands. He had not deserved such a death.

"We captured several of his ferals to find out where Vlad went," Szabina said. "But their minds are closed to us."

"We know where he is."

It was Jonathan who spoke up. He had been standing in the back of our group, hovering by the doorway, but he now moved to the front.

"I am in the process of transformation. I am linked to Ilona through her blood. You can use me to track her. They are in London, I am quite certain of it."

"Then we must make haste," Anara said, wiping at her eyes and shooting to her feet in a rapid move. "We must leave at once."

"We cannot be rash, Anara," Szabina said gently. "We planned for the attack on the fortress, and still lost our leader and many of our own. Vlad and his sister know that we are after them. They will have many more of their followers in London."

"Then we assemble various groups," Anara swiftly rejoined. "We can send a wire to allies of

Radu to help us—I know they are still out there. They will join us."

"We can't just go to London," Seward said, frowning. "A group of bloody vampires entering the city en masse for a battle will cause such panic that—"

"I do not care about the human population!" Anara cried. "They will soon all be very aware of our existence if Vlad even partially succeeds. It was only a matter of time before our war bled into your world."

"We do not have the numbers, nor do we have time to organize and recruit more allies," Abe added, rubbing his temples.

"Then what do you propose?" Anara demanded. "The longer we wait to attack, the more difficult it will be to locate them. They may not even remain in London."

In the space of silence that followed, an idea took root in my mind. It was a relatively simple solution, but terrifying and dangerous. *The best ideas are the dangerous ones,* Father had once told me. *Always. Mister Darwin did not release* **On the Origin of Species** *for years because he knew it contained the most dangerous ideas. And look at what happened when he published it. He changed the world.*

My idea, though risky, could possibly save the world. I moved forward until I was in the center of the room.

"We need to set a trap," I said. "I agree that we should not confront them in London—too many human lives would be at risk. We need to lure them away from London rather than pursue them like we did before. Jonathan, you pointed out vacant estates in and around London to Vlad. Is there an estate outside of London where we can meet them? Somewhere relatively isolated?"

"There is a vacant estate in Purfleet, called Carfax," Jonathan said hesitantly, his features taut with worry. "But, Mina—"

"How do you propose we lure them?" Anara interrupted, looking at me with incredulity.

"We give them what they want. I'm the daughter of one of the last human members of the Order of the Dragon. Jonathan and I will convince them that we want to join their side. I'll swear allegiance to Vlad and vow to destroy the Order from within. When they come to us at the estate in Purfleet, we'll kill them. Their followers will scatter and the newly infected will die with them."

"Mina," Jonathan breathed, shaking his head. "That is not—"

"It has to be us who set the trap, Jonathan. Ilona is obsessed with you. She's already affected your mind once; it's not without reason that you've fallen sway to her. And Vlad has to be obsessed with destroying the Order; they nearly succeeded in killing him once," I said.

"It will not work. You'll never convince them

of your defection," Anara protested. "Vampires can sense deception. Vlad is responsible both directly and indirectly for the deaths of your parents. You won't be able to conceal your hatred for him. The Order of the Dragon has disbanded. There has not been an organized meeting for years—it's no longer a threat to Vlad."

"He thinks it is still a threat. When I confronted him in the fortress, he told me that the Order and I are too late to stop him. As . . . as for my deception," I continued, bracing myself for the reaction to my next statement. "There's a very simple way of convincing them I'm telling the truth."

"What is that?" Anara asked suspiciously, her eyes narrowed.

"I undergo the transformation Jonathan is going through now," I said, struggling to keep my voice steady. "I become vampire."

11

THE BLOOD

The room erupted into a chorus of protests.

"Mina, this is madness!" Abe shouted. "You cannot be serious. You do not know what effect such a transformation will have on you."

"You cannot put your life at such risk," Jonathan agreed. "We will find another way."

"No, Mina," Gabriel said furiously. "How can you even suggest such a thing?"

"You could die," Szabina added. "Are you willing to take such a risk?"

"Listen to me, all of you," I said, raising my voice above the continued protests and murmurs of incredulity. "If we use one of the captured feral vampires to . . . to drain me and feed me their blood, I'll be connected to Vlad as they are. We have seen with Jonathan—and other humans—that it can take weeks or longer for the transformation to complete. I don't need to be in the process of transformation for very long, only a day or two, until we confront and kill Vlad and Ilona. We can then kill the feral, and release us both from vampirism. I won't be able to convince Vlad that I want to join them if I'm not in the process of becoming vampire."

"Mina," Abe's face was still pale with anxiety, "I acknowledge that your plan is a sound one, but there is no guarantee it will work. You heard Szabina. They have not yet been able to communicate with Vlad through the ferals. Why add even more risk to an already precarious enterprise?"

"We have already tried ambushing them," I replied. "They're expecting us to do so again, and they'll be prepared. They won't expect us to join them. Luring them to us is our best chance of defeating them. Once Vlad and Ilona are dead, their followers will most likely scatter, and the ones who have been recently infected will be released from vampirism as well."

My words did not seem to reassure Jonathan, Abe, or Gabriel, who still looked worried. But Anara, Szabina, and even Seward, seemed slightly more convinced. The remaining vampires looked dubious.

"The transformation gravely affects your mind," Szabina said finally. "It affects everyone differently. There is no way to predict how it will affect you. Even if you are under the influence of the Blood for a brief period, you will have to fight for your sanity. You will have to welcome your own darkness without letting it consume you."

Icy fingers of dread crept up my spine at her words. I thought of what the transformation had done to Lucy and Jonathan. Its effect on me would indeed be unpredictable. But I held firm. I had to look past my fear if I was going to kill Vlad and Ilona.

"I know this comes with great risk . . . and it may not work. But I worry that if we do not stop them in London, it'll be too late."

"Mina's plan is risky, but it may work," Anara said, turning to address the others. "Our numbers are small, and time is against us, so we must all be in agreement. Are there any dissenters?"

Again, I was surprised that Anara was helping me, even siding with me. It was hard to believe this was the same creature who had nearly killed me on two separate occasions. I could only assume that it was desperation that propelled her—she fiercely wanted Vlad's death.

"Mina," Jonathan spoke up, moving towards me, his hazel eyes shot with anxiety. "Szabina is quite right about the effect the transformation has on your mind. Look at what I am going through."

"It will be temporary," I insisted, taking his hands. I was relieved that he was speaking to me, and he did not pull away my touch. "For both of us. Once Vlad and Ilona are dead, and we mercifully kill the feral who transformed me, we'll both be released from vampirism. Many will be released. I believe this is the best way to end this nightmare."

Jonathan lifted my hands to his, kissing them, and I felt a soothing rush at the feel of his lips on my skin.

"How could I have not known how very brave you are?" he whispered, his face infused with both worry and admiration. "Very well. I will go along with your plan."

THE FERAL VAMPIRE lunged towards me, barely restrained by the shackles that chained her to the cellar wall. She was petite, with matted red hair and pitch black eyes that were hungrily trained on my throat. Despite her small size, she exuded great strength, and terror flooded me as I made myself stand stock-still.

I was now standing in the cellar, protectively flanked by Szabina, Anara, Gabriel, Abe, and Seward. Though they were all silent, I could feel their tension.

Before we had made our way down to the cellar, Jonathan approached and embraced me. I leaned in to him, relieved that he had not kept his distance from me as he'd vowed to in Transylvania.

His eyes were wet with tears, and he confessed that it would be too difficult for him to watch the feral drink from me. Anara and Szabina had then pulled me aside to prepare me for what was to come.

"I have the ability to control feral vampires. They are newly transformed and susceptible to hypnosis—not only from their maker, but from other vampires. Radu taught—" Anara's voice caught as she spoke her maker's name, and pain darted across her features before she continued. "Radu taught me how to do it years ago. It only works in our tongue. But the hypnosis does not always take. We were fortunate that it worked in the fortress," she warned. "The feral will drain you of your blood. Under my guide, it will bite its wrist and press it to your lips. You will barely be conscious, and instinct will make you drink. You will then go into a deep sleep. When you awaken, the transformation will have already begun."

I tried to maintain my calm, but trepidation filled me at the thought of the feral draining me of my blood.

Now that I stood opposite the feral, I felt my courage slip and panic began to rise. What if it completely drained me and I did not survive the transformation? What if I was unable to properly function during my transformation and was reduced to hisses and growls, like Lucy?

"If you want to change your mind, now is the time to tell us," Szabina said, studying me closely.

"No," I forced myself to say, swallowing back my apprehension as I gave her a nod. "I'm ready."

Anara approached the feral, kneeling down to address her in that same melodic language she had used at the fortress. The feral immediately calmed, going silent as she sank down to the floor in a crouch, her predatory eyes still trained on me.

Szabina gently took me by the hand and guided me forward. I took steady breaths to remain placid as we approached the now stoic feral, who continued to track my approach with her black eyes.

"You may want to close your eyes," Szabina whispered. "It will make this easier."

I obliged without protest. With my eyes closed, I did not have to look into the soulless eyes of the feral eager to feast on my blood. I could now only hear the faint breaths of the others as Szabina continued to guide me forward, seating me on the floor with my back pressed against the stone wall.

I did not know how close I was to the feral, but I could hear her sharp, guttural breaths somewhere in my vicinity. My pulse quickened and I clenched my quaking hands in my lap in an attempt to still them. I became very aware of the sound of the feral's breathing, my own uneven breaths, and the tense silence of the room.

It happened quickly. There was a hot breath

on my neck and the piercing of sharp fangs into my throat's fragile flesh. Instinctively, I cried out and tried to move away, but Szabina's hands held me still as the creature eagerly drank from me, and my nausea swelled as my blood flowed into her hungry mouth. Again, I tried to move away, but Szabina continued to hold me still. The time to change my mind had passed.

I grew increasingly weak as my blood drained from my body, and a lethargy more powerful than I had ever known took hold of me. I struggled to hold on to my consciousness, but I was claimed by an abrupt yet calming blackness.

Soon, I was floating in that strange space between consciousness and dreams, and memories flickered through my mind like photographic images come to life.

I was a child of five, giggling as my mother chased me through the house, to the great annoyance of my governess. I stood alone in Highgate Cemetery, my small body racked with sobs as I stood over my mother's grave. I was a child of ten, seated on the floor of Father's study as I completed a biological sketch of a butterfly, eagerly holding it up for his inspection. He took off his spectacles to examine it before giving me a wide approving smile and a nod.

I was a girl of fifteen, hurrying down the hallway, eager to discuss the book I had just read with Father. I halted in my tracks at the sight of a hand-

some young man with wavy chestnut hair and cerulean blue eyes standing outside his study. **Young Mister Van Helsing**, *Father boomed, approaching him with a smile. The man returned the smile, and a rush of warmth filled me when his eyes met mine. I was a young woman, walking through the streets of Amsterdam with Abe. He stopped mid stride and quite suddenly pulled me into his arms, his mouth gentle against mine as we kissed. Abe and I were lying beneath the stars in a forest clearing, our bodies lovingly entwined, flushed with love.*

I stood opposite a police officer, frantically trying to explain what I had seen, my words catching on sobs.

Some kind of man—monster—feasted on my father! *I screamed.* **I saw it—you saw the marks on his neck! You must do something! Please!**

I stood over Father's grave. Abe stood next to me, and I pressed his engagement ring firmly into his palm, turning to walk away from him as he called out my name, ignoring the searing pain in my chest.

I hovered on the edge of a ballroom, filled with both grief and loneliness. Another handsome man with dark hair and dancing hazel eyes approached me, and I felt dormant emotions stir as our eyes met.

I sat in a carriage with Jonathan. The rain

pounded furiously around us, but my entire being was focused on Jonathan. He was looking at me with hopeful anticipation, with so much love. **Yes**, *I whispered to him.* **With all my heart, yes**. *And then his lips were pressed against mine, and I wanted nothing more than to remain in that perfect moment.*

Jonathan and I were at the Langham, dancing the waltz. I felt warm and safe in his arms, and rested my head against his chest.

I was alone. The ballroom and Jonathan vanished, and I stood in a forest clearing in Transylvania. Ahead of me, I could see Vlad and Ilona feasting on my dead parents, their eyes lifeless and empty, their mouths open in permanent screams. I was frozen in horror at the sight, but my surroundings changed once more.

I was in the church where Jonathan and I had married, only now I wore an elaborate ivory wedding dress, drenched with my parents' blood. Jonathan stood before me, his eyes cold and black as he lunged towards me, his lips curled back to reveal fangs.

I opened my mouth to scream, but I was now walking through a bustling village with a basket of vegetables, catching the eye of a young man with curly brown hair and bright green eyes who smiled at me. Feeling suddenly shy, I returned his smile.

The young man was kissing me as we stood in a forest clearing, and I was consumed by desire. He pulled back with great reluctance, resting his lips on my forehead, asking me when I was going to tell our parents, when were we going to be wed? ***I want to be with you always, my love****, he whispered.* ***Always. Soon****, I promised him, my heart bursting with love.* ***Soon.***

It was night. I was lying in a small bed, and Vlad hovered over me. His cold hand was pressed against my mouth as I tried to scream, and his fangs were descending towards my throat.

Silence*, he hissed, his eyes flashing with warning.* ***Lie very still. You will be mine soon. You will be with the rest of us.***

Outside, I could hear the horrified screams of the other villagers, but I was too weak to move as Vlad's fangs sunk into my throat, silencing my attempt at a scream, and I could only lie helpless as he drained me of my blood, until there was only oblivion.

12

TRANSFORMATION

When I opened my eyes, I was lying in a massive bed in an ornate master bedroom, similar to the guest room I'd rested in back in Budapest.

A worried looking Abe sat at my bedside. Anara, Szabina, and Gabriel stood behind him, while Seward hovered by the doorway. They all looked starkly relieved when I opened my eyes.

"How long have I been sleeping?" I croaked, sitting up. I felt heavy and lethargic, as if I had been sleeping for days.

"For several hours. It is just after sunset," Anara replied. "What type of dreams did you have? Were there any that may have come from the feral?"

"Perhaps we should ask how she is feeling before interrogating her," Abe said, glaring at

Anara before turning back to me. "Are you feeling ill at all? Weak?"

"Just tired," I groggily replied, rubbing my eyes. "My dreams . . . they were like memories. Events from my past. Twisted versions of them. There . . . there were also nightmares. Horrible images," I recalled with a shudder as I thought of the sight of Vlad and Ilona feasting on my parents. "And yes, there were also memories that were not my own," I added, thinking of the young man in the village, his kiss, and the image of Vlad hovering over me, his sharp fangs descending towards my throat. Snatched memories from the female vampire who had drank from me—a life that had been tragically lost.

"Then you are sharing memories with the feral," Szabina said, looking relieved. "You should soon have a direct connection to Vlad. We will have to prepare you for when your mind is linked with his. Vlad's influence is strong, like his sister's. You have seen her influence on your husband."

"Where is Jonathan?" I asked, frowning as I looked around the room. I knew he hadn't wanted to see the feral drain me, but I hoped he would be at my side for the aftermath, even with the lingering tension between us.

At my question, everyone fell silent. Abe tactfully avoided my gaze, while Szabina and Anara exchanged a look. Gabriel and Seward just looked uncomfortable.

"He was here earlier," Szabina said finally. "He is downstairs in the drawing room with the others."

I could tell that they were hiding something from me, and I started to press, but Abe spoke up.

"Mina needs more rest before you start training her mind," he said to Anara and Szabina. "We are leaving for London early tomorrow. There is plenty of time to prepare her on the journey."

"We need all the time we have, Abraham," Anara said. "Which means we start tonight."

"Mina has just undergone a great—" Abe began, his voice rising.

"Abe," I interrupted. "It is all right. I agree with Anara. We do need to make use of all the time we have."

"Eat something first. And please let me examine you," he grudgingly relented.

After Abe examined me, finding no overt effects of the transformation as of yet, he and the others left the room, and I was left alone with Anara and Szabina.

"Why did Jonathan leave?" I asked bluntly.

"While you were dreaming, you kept murmuring both Jonathan and Abraham's names," Anara said, after a brief pause. "Jonathan left the room after your fifth mention of Abraham's name."

"Oh, no," I whispered, my face flushing hot with embarrassment at the thought.

"Your desires—however deep, however hidden—all come out when you are in the state of transformation. It is like a snake shedding its skin . . . a way of leaving your human side behind as you become vampire. It happens to all of us who undergo the Change," Szabina said.

"You love them both," Anara said plainly. "Why are you trying to hide it?"

"Anara," Szabina said with a frown. "That is none of our concern."

"Why are you even bothering to help me?" I demanded, deftly changing the subject as I glared at Anara. "I know you hate me. You've tried to kill me twice."

"I do not care about you enough to hate you. My father wanted to help you—I am merely honoring his wishes. But most importantly, I want his children dead," Anara calmly replied, not at all perturbed by my words. She could tell that I was evading the issue, and continued. "Do not hide from what's in your mind, Mina. Vlad and Ilona will sense everything. To truly deceive them you must be transparent. You and your husband smell nothing like each other. I assume Jonathan has not shared the marital bed with you."

"Szabina is right—that is none of your concern!" I protested, flushing.

"For your plan to work, it is my concern. Vampires can smell and sense everything. If you are to present yourself as a married couple to Vlad and Ilona, you need to smell like one. And that means sharing a bed."

"It may be helpful that we do not smell of each other," I stammered. "Ilona is obsessed with Jonathan, and jealous of me."

"Then you will need to convince her that you don't mind sharing. Our mating rules are not as stringent as humans are; we often have many mates. For the sake of your plan, you and Jonathan are a married human couple on the verge of transforming into vampires who want to join the winning side. This is your plan, Mina. Now you must follow it through."

"She is right," Szabina quietly conceded. "If Vlad and Ilona sense any tension between you and your husband . . ."

I bit back an angry retort as the truth of their words sank in. It would be quite suspicious if Jonathan and I had any outward friction between us when we presented ourselves to them.

"All right," I said warily. "I will talk to Jonathan. Let's get on with the training . . . I have no appetite."

Szabina gently guided me out of bed and into a plush armchair by the window. She sat down on the chair opposite me, making me close my eyes as she put me under hypnosis.

But as the hypnosis set in, I felt nothing, only a heavy fatigue. When she drew me out of it, frustration swept over me.

"I feel nothing other than this fatigue. It feels like there has been no change in me at all," I said, worried that the transformation would not take hold. We were leaving tomorrow, and there was no alternative plan.

"It takes time. You were only drained and given blood several hours ago," Szabina said, giving my hand a comforting squeeze before getting to her feet. "You do need more rest."

Anara reluctantly agreed, and they left me alone to sleep. Despite my fatigue, I remained awake, still disturbed from what I had seen during my state of unconsciousness, and terrified of what I would see should I fall into it again.

As I was finally drifting off, the bedroom door swung open, and Jonathan entered. I immediately sat up, giving him a tentative smile. But my hope dissipated as I took in his countenance. He held himself rigidly, and his eyes were once again cold and guarded.

"Jonathan—" I began, deciding to address what had happened during my dreams. I got out of bed to approach him, but he held up his hand.

"I do not want to discuss it, Mina," he said wearily. "Anara informed me that we need to appear unified if we are to deceive Vlad and Ilona. We need to sleep next to each other tonight."

He moved past me towards the bed, still avoiding my gaze as he sat down and removed his shoes. It was as if his earlier tenderness towards me had never happened at all.

"I cannot help what I saw in my dreams," I said. "They were like memories. You know what it is like—you're going through the same thing! This isn't going to work if you treat me with such coldness, Jonathan."

I was talking about more than the plan to kill Vlad and Ilona, and I could tell that he understood my meaning. His shoulders stiffened, but he still did not turn around.

"I know you cannot help what you see when you undergo the transformation," he replied. "But you forget that my mind is still not my own, and I can still see the images that Ilona put into my thoughts. Hearing you say his name repeatedly has only made matters worse."

"I told you, you need to fight. You need to use your love for me as a barrier to keep the darkness away. It is the only way we'll succeed."

Jonathan remained silent, and my entire body deflated. Had I truly lost him? Even if my plan to kill Vlad and Ilona worked, how could things ever go back to the way they were before? The weight of the day's events—the feral vampire at my throat, my dark dreams, the impending danger that awaited us in London, and Jonathan's renewed coldness settled over me, and my eyes burned with tears. I turned away from him, pressing my hand to my mouth to stifle a sob.

But I soon felt gentle hands on my shoulders. Jonathan turned me around to face him, his face grave with regret and sorrow as he pulled me into his arms.

"I do not deserve you, Mina," he whispered into my hair, sounding bereft. "Forgive me. Forgive my jealousy. I curse the monster who has done this to us. I will happily destroy her. I am trying to fight the darkness, my darling. I will continue to try."

He took my hand and guided me towards the bed, pulling me down next to him and enfolding me into his arms.

"You need to take the advice you gave me. You have been through much these past few days," he whispered. "Rest, darling. Sleep."

I obliged, my lingering fatigue now seeping in to every part of my body, and my eyes fluttered shut. Jonathan continued to hold me close as I drifted off to sleep, whispering words of endearment into my ear. The sleep I fell into was heavier than any sleep I had ever known, filled with snatches of memory both familiar and strange.

I awoke with a start. The space where Jonathan had lain beside me was now empty, and the early morning rays of dawn streamed past the heavy velvet curtains into the room. I blinked, turning away from the window. The faint sunlight seemed exceedingly bright, and I realized that I felt different. I felt . . . more.

I could clearly hear snatches of conversation

coming from downstairs, when the day before I'd been unable to hear past this room. Outside, I could hear two street vendors bickering in the central square. I could see every intricate detail of the patterns woven into the rugs on the floor and in the curtains. From the kitchen, I could smell freshly baked bread, the sweetness of fruits, and the heavy aroma of coffee. I could also smell the musk of sweat and the coppery scent of blood from the other human and vampire occupants of the house. It seemed as if all of my senses had come to life, and I was truly experiencing them for the first time.

Shaking, I reached up to feel my teeth. They were sharper and more elongated than before. As I touched them, I felt a whisper in the back of my mind, like the soft caress of a lover, firm and insistent.

The end is the beginning, my children. The world will be ours.

It was a coldly familiar voice. It was Vlad's voice.

13

RAGE

"I have never seen the transformation take hold so swiftly," Szabina said with a worried frown, examining the pallor of my skin and my sharpened teeth. "It usually takes much longer for any physical changes to occur."

After hearing Vlad's voice in my mind, I shouted for help, and everyone came into the bedroom at once. I was now seated on the armchair by the window as Szabina examined me. Abe, Jonathan, and the others hovered around us.

"Then we need to stop it before it progresses further," Jonathan said, his voice firm. "Kill the feral now."

"Yes," Gabriel said, practically shaking with worry. "I'll do it."

"I agree," Abe said. "It is too much of a risk to—"

"No," I interrupted. "If I'm hearing him in my

mind, I can communicate with him and lure him to Purfleet. We arrive in England tomorrow—that's only another day."

"Mina—" Jonathan protested.

"I can endure this for another day," I insisted, before turning towards Szabina. "Do I still have time before the transformation is complete?"

"You do," Szabina replied, but she looked uncertain as her vivid eyes roamed over my face. "From the way you look, perhaps two or three days at the most."

"Then another day in this state will do me no harm," I said, though I had to suppress my own trepidation as I got to my feet. The thought of becoming permanently vampire terrified me, but I was determined to carry out my plan. It was the only chance we had and the time for our confrontation was almost at hand.

Everyone looked trepidatious, especially my husband, Gabriel, and Abe; but they reluctantly nodded in agreement. They all filed out of the room so that I could wash and change, except for Jonathan. We kept silent, but I sensed his eyes on me as I washed and put on a dark red traveling dress that Anara had loaned me from one of the wardrobes in the house. As I dressed, I was intensely aware of every sight, smell and sound— the brightness of the sunlight filtering in the window, the voices from downstairs and outside,

Jonathan's overwhelming scent of honey, blood, and oak.

"Mina," he said, when I finished getting dressed, approaching me to cup my face in his. I hungrily took him in; with my heightened vision, he looked even more handsome. His pale skin gleamed like fine ivory, his hazel eyes a vivid green speckled with gold, his mouth sensually full. I could even sense his emotions—love, worry, fear.

"I know how you are feeling. It is as if the entire world has come alive around you."

"Yes," I whispered. "I can feel everything."

"I know it is difficult, but try not to let it overwhelm you."

I gave him an agreeable nod, and moved over to the mirror to put on my veiled hat.

"Perhaps . . . perhaps you shouldn't look at your reflection," Jonathan hedged.

But it was too late. I had already glimpsed my reflection. My skin was ghostly pale, my eyes shimmered like golden fire, and my lips were red and flushed with blood. Though I was not yet fully transformed, I already looked like one of those monsters.

Jonathan watched me with concern as I hastily turned away from the mirror, putting on the veiled hat that concealed my face. I gave him another nod to indicate that I was all right, though I was still shaken by my appearance.

As we descended the stairs to join the others, I

tried to steel myself against the multitude of smells and sounds that seized my senses. When we reached the front entrance hall at the base of the stairs, I could even feel the emotions of the other humans and vampires in the house, as powerfully as any scent or sound. There was anxiety, tension, and great distress.

I halted in my tracks, overwhelmed. How could I hope to confront Vlad and Ilona when I felt so deluged by my heightened senses?

"Try to focus on one thing at a time; that has helped me," Jonathan said gently, taking my hand. "Focus on the feel of my hand in yours."

I heeded his advice, focusing on the coolness of his hand over mine as we made our way to the dining room, where the others were gathered.

I took everyone in when we entered the room, as I had barely paid attention to any of them when Szabina was examining me. Gabriel appeared to me just as he had before, darkly beautiful, his silver eyes glittering. Seward also looked the same, though his boyish features appeared slightly more pronounced.

But like Jonathan, Abe seemed even more handsome to me now, his blue eyes more vivid, his wavy chestnut hair shot with gold as it caught the light, his lean muscles pronounced beneath the crisp white shirt and dark vest he wore. I was unable to suppress the jolt of desire that shot through me at the sight of him, and I had to avert my eyes. If Jonathan sensed the emotion, he made no indication of it, taking the seat next to me as I tried to eat. Thankfully, I did not yet feel a desire for blood, but the plate of fresh bread and fruit did not entice my appetite. I still forced myself to eat, though the food was tasteless in my mouth.

"We have time before the train leaves," Szabina spoke up. She was studying me with concern; no doubt my struggle to acclimate myself to my awakened senses were evident. "Perhaps Mina should take more time to adjust before we depart."

Everyone's eyes turned towards me, and I flushed. They all nodded in agreement, my husband and Abe enthusiastically so.

"Wilhelmina," Szabina said, giving me a gentle smile. "Shall we take a walk? Your husband can accompany us as well. It will be good to get you acclimated to your new senses."

Moments later, the three of us, and two vampire guards who followed us from a distance, left the house to make our way down the bustling street.

At first, the array of senses that hit me were too much, and I felt myself reeling. Sounds that I had long ago grown accustomed to—horse hooves clattering on cobblestoned streets, vendors shouting about their wares, even the conversations around me—seemed to reverberate around me. As we walked, I could hear the details of an argument a couple were having inside a home, the distant peal of laughter from a child, even the whispered words of what sounded like two clandestine lovers in a bedroom.

A cacophonous array of blood, copper, and sweat hit my nostrils, while every visual detail of the street around me was amplified—the color of the houses, the detail of cobblestone patterns, the vivid blue of the sky.

"It took me a full year to adjust to my heightened senses," Szabina said, studying my face with concern. "This is just what you're seeing as you go through your transformation. If you were to complete the transformation, everything would be even more vivid."

"It's . . . it's too much," I whispered, stopping as Jonathan grasped my shoulder. "I don't know if—"

"We can kill the feral and end this now," Jonathan said swiftly. "Say the word, and we will do it."

I closed my eyes, but Jonathan already had my arm in a firm grip as he began to lead me back to the house. But I remembered all that was at stake—the human lives in London, Europe— the world.

"No," I said, but Jonathan kept dragging me along. "Jonathan. No."

He stopped and turned to face me, his mouth set in a grim line.

"I can adjust," I whispered, turning to look at

Szabina, who gave me a smile that was edged with worry. "Let's continue."

I turned and continued to make my way down the street, taking deep breaths to maintain my calm. I took Jonathan's earlier advice and focused on one thing at a time rather than allow my senses to be assaulted all at once, and gradually, I felt myself relaxing. We made it as far as the train station before turning back to head back to the house. I could feel Szabina and Jonathan's eyes trained on me the whole time. Once we reached the house, Szabina gave me a broad smile. She looked relieved.

"You did well, Wilhelmina," she said. "You must rest now. Your senses have endured much these past few hours. We must be careful not to overwhelm you."

As we entered, Abe and Seward were emerging from the drawing room, and at the sight of Abe, I had to force myself to quell a sudden burst of longing; I'd felt a minor version of it before, but the power of it was so great that I almost stumbled back. Jonathan stiffened at my side, but kept his grip firm on my arm as he led me upstairs to the bedroom.

"Rest," he said, his tone hovering between polite and curt, before he left the room.

Somehow, I managed to rest, quelling my restless senses by closing my eyes and focusing on the steady sound of my breathing, the rush of blood through my veins. It seemed as if not much time had passed before Gabriel had come up to my room to fetch me.

"May I ask you something?" he asked, as we made our way out of the room and down the hall towards the stairs.

"Yes," I replied, with a curious frown.

"How is it different? I've always been this way," he confessed.

"It's as if everything was dull and muted," I said, after a brief pause. "And now . . . there is nothing but color. But it is all difficult to adjust to . . . like looking directly into the sun."

Gabriel studied me curiously before giving me a small nod. When we reached the top of the stairs, he reached out to grasp my arm.

"Vlad and Ilona are monsters. When one of them is in your mind, try not to forget who you are."

"Of course," I replied, baffled, but he held my gaze for several long moments before proceeding down the stairs.

It took great effort, but by the time we left the house and arrived at the train station, I managed to somewhat acclimate myself to my increased awareness without allowing it to overwhelm me.

We boarded the first train of the day to Budapest, taking up several different compartments around the train to avoid attracting too much attention from the other passengers, who would no doubt take notice of so many unnaturally tall and beautiful men and women.

When we switched trains to board the Orient Express in Budapest, I felt a great sadness that I realized was caused by the memory of Radu. I would always associate the city with the compassionate creature I had known so briefly, who had given his life to help us destroy his children. As I had long ago linked Amsterdam with Abe, Budapest would always be synonymous with Radu.

The Orient Express was the finest train I had ever traveled on, and Anara had arranged for our group to have our own sleeping carriage. With my perceptive vision, the gilded drapery, leather chairs, velvet curtains, and mahogany paneled interior seemed even more resplendent. I could only assume that Anara had inherited Radu's wealth for her to afford such accommodations.

But there was no time to appreciate the luxury of the train. Jonathan and I settled into our compartment, but as soon as the train pulled out of the station for the long journey to Paris, we went to find Anara and Szabina.

Both Anara and Szabina were in the compartment next to ours, and they separated us to begin our training. Szabina led Jonathan back to our compartment, while I remained with Anara.

Once we were alone, Anara sat down opposite

me, fixedly holding my eyes, and I was reminded of Radu's intense gaze.

"When I first became vampire, my rage and hatred towards humans was strong. Radu's love managed to pull me away from those emotions, but they remained beneath the surface. I felt that hatred when Gabriel brought you and your friends into our home. You radiated with fear, and I have experienced the very worst of human fear. It made me react violently," she said. Her words were not an apology, and she spoke with frankness. "I'm telling you this because it is rage that you need to convince Vlad. He is all rage—no love. It is what he understands; it is what drives him. I believe there is rage in you, Mina. But you are a good person," she added, the statement sounding more like a denunciation than regard. "Your goodness makes you suppress, rather than embrace, your rage. Gabriel told Radu that you nearly killed him when he revealed himself to you."

I lowered my eyes, flushing with shame at the memory.

"Yes. But that was when I thought all vampires were monsters, and I did not know if I could trust him. It wasn't—"

"Your reaction proves that you are capable of allowing your rage to drive you. For the next two days, you need to embrace your rage, as you did when you nearly killed your brother. That is how you'll connect to Vlad and lure him. Who else do you feel anger towards?"

"My parents," I whispered, after a long pause. It felt like a betrayal to admit it aloud, but it was true. "They kept many secrets from me."

"Good," Anara said, looking pleased. "That will be your reason for joining them. Your parents betrayed you. In a way, they both abandoned you. What about your life in London? Besides Jonathan, was there anyone you were close to? What about enemies?"

There was Clara, of course, but she was my sole ally. I thought of Mary Harker, Jane Newton, Horace Welling, and the rigid society men and women who had been so cruel to my Father and attempted to shun me.

"I was a bit of an outcast," I said hesitantly. "But the snobbery of London society is hardly enough—"

"It is everything. Humans have been cruel to you. They do not deserve your loyalty. Focus on the cruelest things they've done to you, and use it. When you speak to Vlad in your mind, focus on your rage towards them. All of them."

A part of me wanted to protest, to defend my parents; especially my father. But I did need to convince Vlad that I wanted to join him, and any persistent loyalty towards my parents would dissuade him from believing me.

"Tell him that you know where the last members of the Order are hiding. That will entice him," Anara continued. "And remember, you want to lure him out of London and to the estate in Purfleet. When you are ready, close your eyes, and focus on your breathing."

I obliged her as she put me under hypnosis, as Szabina had done the night before, and closed my mind off to my surroundings. Soon, the sound of the wheels on the train tracks and the murmured voices of the others in neighboring compartments faded into nothing.

"Search for Vlad's whisper in your mind. Speak back to him, as if he were in this carriage with us. And do not forget your rage towards your parents and other humans—their betrayal, their cruelty."

I kept my eyes tightly shut, listening intently for the whisper I'd heard when I first awoke. After several long moments, I heard it. It was faint at first, and gradually became clear.

The world will be ours, my children. Make your own progeny. Feast and multiply.

The words repeated themselves like a litany, and I had to set aside the revulsion that flared in my chest at the sound of his voice in my mind, at the horror of his words. Instead, I allowed his words to flow through me. And I spoke back.

I am the last Ghyslaine. One of the last

members of the Order of the Dragon. I want to join you. I pledge my fealty to you.

I repeated the words over and over again, until I felt a strange pull, as if I was being beckoned. There was a presence in my mind; I felt it as clearly as if Vlad were seated next to me in the carriage.

I had his attention. He was listening to me.

It is I, Wilhelmina Ghyslaine. I have failed in my attempt against you. I have become vampire like my husband. I no longer belong in the human world. They are not worthy of my loyalty. I will wait for you at the Carfax estate in Purfleet. I can help you destroy the Order; I know where they hide.

I felt a sudden hatred, a surge of maleficence that clung to my mind. I did not know if it came from me, or Vlad, but I held firm to my words, repeating them in my mind.

My parents betrayed me. Humans were cruel to me. I never should have fought you. Let me help you destroy the Order. Let me help you win.

I thought of my mother. She could have left the fight against Vlad to the other members of the Order. She did not have to abandon me. My father could have told me what he was doing in Transylvania. They had chosen to put their pursuits above their daughter, whom they supposedly loved. They had left me, alone and isolated, to shoulder the burden of a dark legacy. Hot rage took hold of me as I continued speaking to him in my mind.

My parents were never worthy of my love. They left me alone. They abandoned me. Let me join you, Master.

"Mina!" Abe cried.

My eyes flew open. I had fallen to the floor of the compartment, and I was lying on my back. Abe was crouched behind me, and he helped me to my feet, his brow furrowed with concern. Anara stood right outside the compartment, her eyes wide with uncertainty.

"Why did you wake me?" I demanded, extricating myself from Abe's grip. "I was speaking to Vlad. He was listening to me!"

"Your eyes went completely black, and you lost consciousness," Anara said. "I called Abraham for help."

"I–I'm quite all right," I stammered, though I was alarmed at her description of my state. "Put me back under hypnosis. I need to keep talking to him."

"No," Anara and Abe said at once.

"You need to rest and eat," Abe said, silencing me before I could protest.

"Then we need to practice separating your dark thoughts from your rational ones," Anara added. "Especially when you are so close to becoming vampire."

I reluctantly fell silent, surprised by the flare of

rage I felt at their words. The darkness was still there, and it was strangely intoxicating. It was difficult to resist its pull, and I had to take several deep breaths to calm myself.

We headed to the dining carriage, where the others were already seated. Both Jonathan and Gabriel rose from their seats when I entered, worriedly searching my face. I gave them a small smile to indicate that I was all right, though I still felt unsettled.

We took the table opposite them, and Jonathan confirmed that he had been able to connect with Ilona. He had also lost consciousness, and it had been very difficult for him to return to himself again. But he had vaguely been able to make out where she was—a large home in London with an interior he recognized.

"I handled the sale last year. It is located in Mayfair and currently vacant. It is one of the houses I told them about during my capture. There were many of those creatures gathered, including Vlad."

"Bloody hell," Seward whispered, closing his eyes. "So they are in London."

After I recounted my own experience of connecting with Vlad in my mind, Szabina frowned.

"This worries me," she murmured. "We cannot risk you both losing hold of your sanity and actually joining Vlad—or revealing your deception."

"I will never forget that they are responsible for the deaths of my parents and many other innocents," I said hotly, offended by the suggestion. "I'll do whatever training is necessary to ensure that I don't lose myself; but we must keep connecting with them. This proves that my plan is working. They're listening to us, and now we know for certain that they're in London. We must continue to lure them to us in Purfleet."

"Vlad and Ilona are powerful," Gabriel said, addressing Szabina and Anara. "Are we certain that Mina and Jonathan can kill them on their own?"

"They won't be alone," Abe interjected. "The rest of us will hide on the grounds of the estate, ready to strike when necessary."

"There is no certainty that we will get to them in time," Szabina added. "Anara and I will do our best to ensure that Mina and Jonathan know exactly what to do when the time comes."

"We'll be ready," I said. I looked forward to killing them both; I could feel my kukri knives rub eagerly against the skin beneath my sleeves. Jonathan did not share my confident look. His eyes were shadowed with trepidation, but he gave the others an affirmative nod.

Szabina and Anara led us to the empty smoking saloon, where we had slightly more space to move, and briefly trained us on the best way to dispatch Vlad and Ilona. While I was familiar with much of what they told us because of the training I had undergone prior to the fortress attack, I could see that Jonathan looked overwhelmed by all the information.

"You can do this," I assured him. "Just remember all that those monsters have put you through."

"I am unable to forget," Jonathan replied darkly.

We were separated to connect with Vlad and Ilona once more. Anara cautioned me to hold on to my true intentions beneath the rage. When she again put me under hypnosis, I embraced the familiar sound of Vlad's whisper in my mind.

But this time, his whispers were personal. He was speaking directly to me. *Mina*, his voice whispered. *Mina*.

It is I, Mina. Let me join you, I responded, pushing away my trepidation at hearing the monster use my name. *I will wait for you at the Carfax estate in Purfleet, and I will help you.*

As I silently spoke to him, I began to think of my mind as two separate entities. The dark and the light. Vampire and human. I held back my true thoughts as I whispered the lies.

Come to me so that I can kill you, you monster, my true thoughts raged. *Come to me so that I can rip out your heart with my blade.*

"When I first saw you," Jonathan said reflectively. "You were sitting off to the side of the ballroom. You were wearing all black, which was quite scandalous to the women who sat near me. They thought it inappropriate to attend a ball when in mourning. You looked unhappy, but there was still something about you that drew me in."

Jonathan and I were now seated on our beds in our compartment. After completing our training with Anara and Szabina, we had taken a brief meal in the dining carriage with the others. Unlike the day before, when fatigue had weighed me down, I now felt a pulsating energy, and I had no desire to rest. I only agreed to try at the urging of Jonathan and the others.

"I think I loved you before I even said a word to you," Jonathan continued now. "But I was such a fool, Mina."

"What do you mean?" I asked. With my newly heightened awareness, I could sense the conflicting emotions emanating from him—love, worry, confusion, resolve.

"To think that life as a member of London society would ever satisfy you, even if it were with me. Now that I have seen what you are capable of, I cannot see you happily living that life. I know this has been a perilous journey, and you have experienced much despair, but I have never seen such passion in you as I have during this journey. It is as if you've come to life."

"You think I want this?" I asked, incredulous, getting to my feet. "Vampires in our midst, on the verge of destroying everything? A possible war that—"

"No," Jonathan said, fervently shaking his head as he also clamored to his feet. "Of course not. But you are a scientist and an adventurer. It is who you are, Mina. I see that now. Once this is over—Vlad and Ilona dead, the threat of vampires gone—do you see yourself happily living in London as if none of this ever happened?"

"Yes!" I cried. The dark rage that I had kept at bay seized me once more. "It is all I have wished for—to have things back to the way they were before your abduction!"

"Being the mother to our children? Hosting charity balls? Afternoon tea with my mother and other society wives?" Jonathan pressed, ignoring my outburst. "Think of it, Mina. That would be your life."

"I have already thought of it," I protested, though my voice wavered, and a familiar dread stirred in my stomach at the picture Jonathan painted of my future in London. "I agreed to marry you, did I not? I *am* married to you. Your life will be my life. As long as you are in it, I will be happy. This is the last thing we should be focused on when we are so close to confronting Vlad and Ilona. We need to be focused on the task that lies before us—not if I will hate having tea with your mother in the future."

Jonathan's conflicted expression remained as his eyes swept over my face. Unlike the day before, or in Transylvania, there was no coldness, anger or jealousy in his eyes—only an acceptance that made me nervous. He leaned forward to place a chaste kiss on my lips.

"You are right. We should rest," he said quietly.

He turned from me, removing his coat and dropping it on the side table. I knew the matter was not settled, and my burgeoning rage swelled. Had I not risked my life to rescue him? Had I not married him?

My hands shot out to grip his arms, forcing him around to face me.

"How can you doubt me—us—after all that I have done for you? After we have been wed? Do you not know what I've gone through, all in the name of rescuing you?" I shouted, furious.

"Mina," Jonathan's voice was panicked. "Please. Come back to yourself."

The genuine fear in his voice pierced my veil of fury. I released him at once, stumbling back. Jonathan looked down at his arms, rolling up his sleeves. There were red marks on his skin from where I had grabbed him. Shaking, I pressed my hand to my mouth.

"Oh, Jonathan. I–I am so sorry," I breathed.

"That was not you. The whites of your eyes went completely black. This frightens me. I worry for you."

"I'm all right," I protested, more loudly than I intended, and Jonathan tensed. I took a breath to calm myself before speaking again. "I'll contain my rage. This is almost over. We are so very close, Jonathan."

Jonathan was silent for a long moment before giving me a grudging nod of agreement. When we lay down next to each other on one of the narrow beds to sleep, he pulled me in close to the warmth of his body. Despite our physical closeness, I could still sense a distance from him, though there was also the unmistakable sense of desire—a desire which he did not act upon—and his slow even breaths told me that he had fallen asleep.

But my increased awareness and renewed energy kept me awake, along with the lingering rage that flowed throughout my body. Soon, I could hear Vlad's distant whisper in my mind, and I welcomed it.

Mina, he whispered. *Mina*.

I am here, Master. Let me join you. Let me help you destroy the Order, I replied, all the while my true thoughts swirled beneath the surface, like a raging inferno.

Let me kill you, monster.

14

PURFLEET

The cliffs of Dover dominated the shore in the near distance, like a massive hand beckoning us home. Jonathan and I stood side by side on the deck of the ferry as it crossed the Channel from France towards Dover. We were finally arriving back in England, but I felt no sense of relief. I knew that Vlad and his followers were here, like creatures who had slithered out of a nightmare and into reality. The day was appropriately ominous—gray and cloudy, storm clouds hovering above, keeping quiet watch over us as we neared the English shore.

Though I was filled with dread over the looming confrontation with Vlad and Ilona, I knew that it was inevitable. It was the only way to stop Jonathan's complete transformation into vampire, and to save the human world. There was no time for doubt or hesitation.

I turned to glance behind me, where the others from our group stood amongst the crowd on the deck. Abe's gaze had been centered on me, but he averted his eyes. The others were somberly watching the approaching coast, their faces taut with anxiety.

During the final stretch of our journey, a heavy silence had fallen over our group. Unlike the attack at the fortress, there was a sense of finality to this confrontation. At the fortress, the lives of Jonathan and the other human prisoners had been at stake. Now it was the fate of the human world. I recalled Vlad's words in my mind with a chill. *Feast and multiply*. If we failed today . . .

"Mina," Jonathan said, pulling me from my dark thoughts as he turned me to face him. "I love you, so very much. After our discussion last night, I do not want you to doubt that. Especially with what we are about to face."

"I know," I said. His words from last night still stung, but there was no time to dwell on them now, and I gave him a forced smile.

When the ferry disembarked at Dover, we made our way to the train station. To avoid suspicion, and in case we were being watched when we arrived in Purfleet, Jonathan and I would travel separately to Purfleet by train, while the rest of our group would take the next train that departed fifteen minutes later. During a brief stop in Paris before we transferred trains, Jonathan had sent a wire to Vlad in Mayfair, providing him with the exact address of the Carfax estate in Purfleet. While I had no doubt that Vlad had heard my telepathic words, we wanted to make absolutely certain that he knew where to find us.

On the platform, we murmured our goodbyes to our vampire allies, and Anara and Szabina approached us, inspecting the weapons we were bringing with us. I had my kukri knives, and we both had wooden stakes doused with wolfsbane tucked securely into our clothes.

"You remember exactly what to do?" Szabina asked anxiously. At our nods, she continued, "We will hide on the outskirts of the estate. As soon as we can, we will join you."

She gave us both a warm embrace. Anara stepped forward, taking both my hands in hers. I studied her warily. I knew Anara was not one for sentiment, and her words were characteristically blunt.

"When the time comes, do not miss, Mina. You miss, you die."

"Anara," Szabina and Gabriel protested, scowling at her.

"Such comforting words," Seward added dryly, as he moved towards us.

"I will not miss," I assured her, and she released my hands, though her eyes were still infused with anxiety.

"It's been a journey, hasn't it?" Seward asked

when Anara stepped back, his countenance now serious. "I'm sorry for doubting you before."

"There is no need for apologies. You have been a great ally. I hope this is not goodbye, no matter what the outcome. I would like for us to remain dear friends."

Seward looked pleased at my request, and nodded his agreement. I stepped forward to give him an impulsive embrace.

"Kill those bloody monsters," he whispered, before pulling away.

It was Gabriel's turn to step forward. His eyes were stormy, his body tense.

"Gabriel," I said, before he could speak. "Please do not try to dissuade me. It is not—"

"I–I wasn't," he stammered, looking genuinely surprised. "Believe me, I will never try to dissuade you again. I just . . . I wanted to say that our mother would be so very proud."

I flushed, feeling guilty for my assumption.

"She would be proud of us both," I whispered, before embracing him.

Abe was now the only one left. He hovered nervously behind the others, staring at some point past my shoulder. Instinctively, I glanced at Jonathan, and he gave me a reassuring nod.

I approached Abe, moving into his arms without a word. His arms encircled me, and I reeled from the emotions that emanated from him. There was overwhelming anxiety, tension . . . and love. The sense of his love was as potent as the sweetest smell, and tears sprang to my eyes. We just held each other for a moment, quietly reveling in the emotions that we both felt but did not speak aloud, even now. When we finally broke apart, Abe met my eyes.

"Mina," he began. It seemed as if there was much he wanted to say, but he murmured just two words. "Stay alive."

The same words I had whispered to him after the train derailment, but now they seemed to mean so much more, seemed to carry so much weight.

"You too," I whispered.

Abe's eyes shifted away from mine, shadowing briefly as they focused on something behind me.

"You should leave. Your husband is waiting."

I turned. Jonathan was standing with the others, pointedly not looking at either of us. I gave Abe one last look, reaching out to clasp his hand, before stepping away to join Jonathan. Jonathan took my hand in his, and we approached the train bound for Purfleet.

When our train pulled away from the station, I turned to watch our group of humans and vampires, who stood on the platform watching us leave. Abe stood separately from the others, his eyes locking with mine and holding them until he faded completely from view, and his words still echoed in my mind. *Stay alive.*

When we arrived at the station in Purfleet, the carriage we had arranged for was waiting for us. Our driver, a man in his fifties with a thin mouth, craggy nose and permanently squinted eyes, took in the pallor of our skin and our worried expressions with so much suspicion that I feared he'd refuse to take us to our destination.

But he did, driving us away from the station and into Purfleet in silence. Purfleet was a quaint town, filled with medieval chalk quarries dotted with winding walkways for visitors, scenic gardens, old seventeenth century buildings, and modern tearooms and hotels for visiting tourists from London. But I could hardly focus on the pleasant sights of the town. My heart pounded with anxiety, my hands trembled in my lap, and my breathing was labored. What if Vlad and Ilona were not at the estate? What if they were? Were we truly prepared to kill them on our own?

"Breathe, Mina," Jonathan whispered at my side, giving my hand a squeeze, though he also looked petrified, and his hand trembled over mine.

I obliged him, and by the time we reached the outskirts of town, I had managed to steady my breathing. The carriage approached a solitary medieval estate that towered at the far end of a long, dusty path. The estate looked as if it had been in disuse for centuries; its brick façade crumbling, the hedges that lined it overgrown, and the surrounding grounds teemed with grasses that had grown wild.

Our driver instinctively seemed to know that danger lay ahead. He abruptly stopped the carriage a dozen yards away from the path that led to the estate's massive front doors.

"I'll leave yer 'ere," he said stubbornly, as if expecting us to argue.

"All right," Jonathan said, his polite tone belying the tension on his face, and he took my hand as we stepped out of the carriage. As soon as we were out, the driver immediately sped away, casting us one last uneasy glance over his shoulder.

Once he was gone, Jonathan tightened his hand over mine, lowering his voice.

"If it becomes necessary, Mina, save yourself. Do you understand?"

"If it becomes necessary, I will save us both."

Jonathan scowled at my response but he did not argue, and kept my hand in his as we turned to head towards the estate. As we made our way down the dusty path, I scanned the dirty cracked windows of the estate to see if anyone observed our approach. But they were empty. The estate appeared to be completely abandoned. Despite my apprehension, I prayed that Vlad and Ilona were inside. Our plan would fail if they were still in London, or had suspected our true intentions.

When we reached the front double doors, I

felt for one of my kukri knives beneath my sleeves, ready to strike if necessary. Jonathan reached out to open the unlocked door, and I held my breath.

The door swung open to a cavernous entrance hall, which must have been grand in its day, but now the wooden floors and vaulted ceilings were scratched and decrepit with age. An inner hall on our right led to a set of rickety stairs, but we moved past it to cautiously move forward, stepping into the first room on our left.

It was a large room that I assumed had once been a drawing room, barren of any furniture and dominated by a sizable window on the opposite end, providing a clear view of the forests that lined the estate's grounds. The oak-paneled walls and fireplace ornately decorated with fine carvings hinted at the gilded room this must have once been.

I entered further, looking around. It was the perfect place to meet Vlad and Ilona. It was close to the front doors, the large window gave us another escape option, and there was a door to close us all in. I prayed that they weren't lying in wait in one of the many other empty rooms of the estate. We were not prepared for an ambush. I used my increased awareness to listen or smell for any other presence in the house. I heard nothing, but I did smell the overwhelming scent of coppery blood.

I stiffened at the scent, recalling something

Jonathan had told me just that morning. *They smell like blood*, he had whispered, looking haunted. *Vampires smell like rage and blood.*

"We can wait for Vlad and Ilona here," Jonathan said abruptly, before I could tell him what I had sensed, his voice abnormally loud. "If any of our former allies follow us, we will kill them where they stand."

I froze, horror racing through me at his words, until I met his eyes and felt his emotions, which screamed with alarm. He was warning me. His hand twitched ever so slightly, gesturing towards the hall outside of the drawing room. *We are not alone*, his eyes told me.

Someone else was here, and they were listening.

"They would be foolish to do such a thing," I replied, holding his eyes to show him that I understood. "They chose not to join us."

"I'm glad we are in agreement," Jonathan said, looking relieved that I had caught on.

My hands trembled as I turned away from him, subtly feeling for my weapons beneath the sleeves and bodice of my dress. Who was watching us? Vlad? Ilona? One of their followers? Regardless of who it was, I knew that I needed to appear calm and resolute. I did not want our voyeur to see my unease, so I kept my eyes focused on the window and away from the door, anxiously waiting for whomever it was to show themselves.

Outside, I could vaguely make out distant figures in the trees that lined the grounds of the estate, and I felt a rush of relief. Abe and the others were here. We weren't alone. I had to will my excitement away, schooling my features into an expression of detached calm.

Behind me, I felt an increased tension from Jonathan, and the sensation of multiple icy eyes on my skin. Praying that my face was an unreadable mask, I turned.

A group of ten vampires entered the drawing room, their furious gazes mostly pinned on me, and though they did not speak, I felt the hiss of *Ghyslaine* in my mind. Though I was not wholly surprised at the presence of other vampires, and we had anticipated this—Vlad would not be foolish enough to come here without protection—I did feel a fissure of alarm. It was crucial that we get the other vampires to leave.

Vlad and Ilona were the last ones to enter. It was eerie to me how human they appeared. Vlad looked like an upper-class English gentleman, with his fine black sack-coat, grey vest and trousers; Ilona a society wife in her midnight blue silk dress. Their dark beauty was the only thing that set them apart from most humans—that and the glittering eyes that shone with suspicion and hatred as they settled on me. *Monsters in human skin*, I thought, recalling Gijs' words. These two creatures were responsible for scores of deaths; including the death of my parents.

But I held my hatred for them at bay, hoping that I looked appropriately reverent as they stepped forward, and forced myself not to flinch at their approach.

Before Jonathan or I could speak, Ilona reached out to grab me by neck, lurching me towards her, her lips curled back to reveal her fangs.

"Jonathan is bound to me. I knew he would come back to his maker," she hissed, as I fruitlessly struggled to release myself from her grip. "My brother tells me you wish to join us. I think you are full of lies."

I watched in mute horror as she swiftly lowered her other hand towards my chest, going directly for my heart. She was going to kill me. I tried desperately to yank myself away from her, but she was far too strong, and Jonathan cried out in alarm, reaching out to attempt to stop her, but it was Vlad who yanked her away from me.

"Not yet, Ilona!"

"I will not listen to her lies!" Ilona snarled, stepping away from her brother to glare at me. "You are a fool to trust her!"

"All that I have told you is true," I said, trying to keep my voice steady. I held onto the black rage that had recently become a part of me, allowing it to color my words as I reverently sank down to my knees. At my side, Jonathan followed suit. "Both of my parents lied to me for my entire life. They betrayed and abandoned me," I continued, quaking with fury as I thought of their treachery. "I have never truly belonged to the human world, I bear it no loyalty. My dear husband is becoming vampire; I have chosen to join him. To join you."

Though my words were lies, the rage behind them were real, and I hoped that they could sense it.

"Tell me what I want to know, and perhaps I will believe you. Tell me where the surviving members of the Order of the Dragon hide," Vlad said, his dark eyes trained intently on me, reminding me much of his father, though his held no traces of warmth or humanity.

I drew myself rigid, my eyes sliding to the other vampires as Jonathan and I climbed back to our feet. They were now regarding me with varying looks of suspicion, surprise, and lingering rage.

"I will only tell you and your sister. This is not information for them," I said, gesturing towards the other vampires.

"You are not in the position to make demands!" Ilona spat, taking a threatening step towards me, but Jonathan moved protectively in front of me.

"Trust needs to be earned on both sides. You both are far stronger than the two of us. We will feel safer delivering this information to you alone," he said, his tone decidedly lawyerly and matter of fact, though I could sense his underlying panic.

Vlad's eyes met mine for several long moments, and I evenly held them, keeping my mind clear.

"I could make you tell me," he said silkily. "We have our ways. I am sure that Jonathan remembers."

"You do not have the time," I said boldly, as Jonathan stiffened at my side, feigning bravery even as terror shot through me at the thought of being tortured at their hands. "You are very close to striking in London. I know that the members of the Order are trying to stop you even now as we speak. My information can help you rid yourself of them."

I saw a brief flare of rage in his eyes at my defiance. Next to me, Jonathan stood rigidly, his body vibrating with anticipation. He was expecting Vlad to strike, but to my great relief, Vlad turned to gesture the other vampires out of the room.

As I watched them file out, the weapons beneath my clothes began to burn against my skin, as if they had somehow come to life and were aching to be buried in the flesh of the monsters before us. We just needed to get close enough to them both and strike at the same time, as we'd practiced. I could feel Jonathan's continued tension; he was like a coiled snake prepared to strike. He was ready.

Once we were alone, my lips curved in a sly smile, and I moved slowly towards Vlad, as Jonathan moved towards Ilona. Vlad remained stock still, his eyes intent on mine, searching for any traces of deception. Ilona looked as if she were going to launch herself at me at any moment, her eyes shifting from me to Jonathan with suspicion.

"Now," Vlad hissed. "Tell me, or I will kill you where you stand."

"The surviving members of the Order are in Constantinople," I said, reciting the information that Anara and Szabina had given me that morning. "That is where they are trying to recruit more followers to destroy you. There are also a dozen members in London right now, trying to prevent your attack."

I nearly screamed as Vlad moved towards me in a flash, his cold hands pressed to the sides of my face, tilting my face up to his. He was searching my mind now. I could feel his presence there, like insects crawling beneath my skin, and I willed the rage to course through me, to keep my mind clear, to not flinch. If he sensed any sliver of deception, I was dead.

After a long and charged moment, he seemed to relax, and his dark eyes went alight with a monstrous hunger.

He believed me. It was time to strike.

"Do you trust me now, Master?" I whispered, angling my arm so that my kukri knife could slide into the palm of my hand. "We kill them, and we wipe out the last threat to you."

But there were sudden shouts of alarm from the entrance hall—it was the other vampires.

"There are others here!"

"She has betrayed you, Master!"

"The Order is here!"

Abe and the others, I realized, panicked. They had been seen.

I heard the front doors crash open, and the mingled scents of Abe and others from our group wafted in. Immediately, the sound of scurrying bodies, snarls, and grunts filled the hall as they began to fight Vlad's vampires.

I was momentarily frozen with terror as Vlad's expression shifted from hunger to an animalistic rage. He was going to kill me. I had to act now.

Moving faster than I thought was even possible, I lifted my kukri and sank the blade into the base of his throat. Dark blood seeped from the gaping wound as I yanked it out, and he stumbled back with a surprised and agonized howl. I raised the blade to sink it into his chest, but he reached out to grab my wrist, his grip so tight that my bones cracked, and as I screamed in pain, I was suddenly in the air, hurled back against the far wall with such force that I nearly lost consciousness, and the room blurred around me.

Out of the corner of my eye, I could dimly see that Jonathan had managed to sink his stake into the side of Ilona's throat, but she now had him pinned to the ground, her face savage with fury as she choked the life from him.

Dazed, my entire body aching with agony, I struggled to get to my feet, but Vlad was instantly in front of me, lifting me up in the air with his hand on my throat, his eyes filled with blazing fury.

"Even if you had succeeded, this does not end with me," he snarled. "I will finish your traitorous line."

He yanked me down towards him, sinking his fangs into my throat. I screamed, but he held me still as he drank from me, draining me of my blood. I would soon lose consciousness. *Think of something,* I thought frantically. *Think.*

But my mind grew increasingly hazy as I was drained, and the edges of my vision began to blur and turn black. There was one last thing I could try—it was the only way I would survive. I felt a miniscule flicker of relief when I saw that he was looking at me as he drank. I weakly met his eyes, probing his mind.

I was stumbling through a forest, dizzy and weak. The flesh of my face and torso was ragged and torn by the cut of their traitorous knives; I was coated with their blood and my own. I sank to my knees and began to crawl, my rage paired with an equal amount of despair. I needed blood or I would die, and I could not allow myself to die. I was the most powerful creature in the world—the Dracula. I had to find a way. But I was too weak to continue moving, and fell onto my bleeding torso, my life's essence draining from me.

I was released as Vlad dropped me and stumbled back, his lips stained with my blood. I swayed weakly, barely able to hold myself upright as my vision swam. Vlad stumbled to his knees, looking ill. Ilona was preoccupied with Jonathan, who had somehow managed to scramble out from beneath her, and she now had him pinned him against the wall.

My hold on consciousness was slipping. I had to strike with my little remaining strength. It would be the last thing I did before leaving this world.

With my vision still blurred and my limbs keening with pain, I managed to reach down into my bodice, yanking out a wooden stake. Vlad's eyes were shut, his hands on his head as he shook violently. I had the perfect angle. The perfect opportunity.

I lifted my arm and launched the stake towards his chest.

You cannot miss, Anara had said. *You miss, you die.*

Time seemed to stand still as the stake flew from my hand and sailed through the air, landing solidly in the center of his chest—right in his heart. Vlad's bellow of pain and fury seemed to shake the entire room, and as his eyes flew open, I removed my other kukri from my sleeve.

This was it. I had no more strength left after this. I hurled the kukri, arching it towards his neck. My eyes met his, and I hoped that he could hear the words that I screamed in my mind, words that I was too weak to speak aloud.

For my parents. Arthur. Lucy. Radu. And scores of other innocent souls.

The blade careened through the air, and when it arrived at its destination, it tore right through the tenuous flesh of Vlad's throat, severing his head from his body, and he fell lifelessly onto the floor.

"NO!"

Ilona's agonized wail pierced the silence, and she launched herself off of Jonathan and towards me, her eyes wild with grief and rage. I stumbled to my knees, too weak to stand or fight, feeling a strangely calm acceptance of my death. Jonathan lay still on the floor behind her, his eyes closed, his chest unmoving. I allowed myself a brief moment of grief for him before meeting Ilona's ferocious eyes. I would go bravely to my death.

Her face was streaked with bloody tears, and when she reached me, she lowered her hand towards my chest. She was going to rip my heart out, and this time she would succeed.

But she abruptly stiffened as a wooden stake

jutted through her chest from behind, her eyes widening in shock and agony. My eyes weakly lifted, and I saw Abe standing behind her. He hurled a knife that lodged solidly in the back of her skull. I watched in a daze as her skin desiccated before my eyes; the pale smooth skin wrinkling, the green eyes turning black, blood seeping from the sockets of her eyes, her nose, her mouth; her true monstrousness finally revealed beneath the shield of her beauty. She slumped sideways to the floor, still and silent.

The others raced into the room behind Abe. In the hallway outside, I could dimly see the dead bodies of the vampires who had come with Vlad and Ilona.

Abe and Gabriel dashed towards me. I was too weak to hear the words they shouted, which seemed so very far away. Abe lifted me in his arms, racing out of the drawing room.

"Burn it down!" someone—Seward?—shouted, and I could smell smoke as Abe dashed with me down the entrance hall and out of the estate.

He kept running until we were on the far edge of the estate grounds, near the towering trees. The world around me had become increasingly dim, and I felt as if I stood on the precipice of consciousness, teetering on the edge, and I had no strength to remain upright.

Abe stumbled to his knees, setting me down on the ground, his face filled with panic and anguish.

He was shouting, but I could only faintly hear his words.

"She is dying! We need help! Mina, my heart, stay with me. Please. Please."

He began to weep as he gazed into my fluttering eyes. I held them, those eyes that I knew and loved so well, glad that they would be the last thing I saw before departing, and I welcomed the darkness that claimed me.

15

GOODBYE

A black void surrounded me.

In the far distance, I could hear the vague murmur of voices, faint as whispers. I felt a powerful yearning to draw closer to them, but I could not move, and the voices continued to drift in and out of my awareness like the ebb and flow of a tide on a faraway shore. I willed myself to concentrate, to hone in on the voices, until one particular voice seemed to rise above the others. It was deeply familiar, and I clung to the steady rise and fall of its cadence, until the words it spoke became clear.

"Robert once told me that he hoped I would always look out for you. He was quite perceptive. I think he knew I loved you before I did. He always had a way of seeing—"

The words faded back into that distant

murmur, becoming unrecognizable once more. I desperately wanted to cry out for the voice to return, to not leave me alone in this place. But more familiar voices came into clarity, and I clung to them like a lifeline.

"You told your first governess you'd no reason ta learn embroidery—you were goin' ta be a scientist li' your father. You made 'a cry . . . 'n you were just a lass o' ten. Any other parent would've been furious, but Robert was only amused. After your third governess quit, he hired your first science tutor. Oh, Mina," the voice continued, beginning to quiver. "Your father'd not want you ta drift away so soon. You'll see your parents again one day, but not yet. Come back t' us, bairn."

"I never should have allowed you to take on those monsters," a different voice said. "I'm unworthy of you, of your love. Mina, I vow to give you your freedom, to allow you to live the life you were always meant to lead, if only you would open your eyes again," the voice broke, dissolving into heartbreaking sobs.

I wanted to respond, but I was paralyzed in the darkness, and silence surrounded me once more. I tried to seek out more voices in the deafening quiet, and I soon heard another familiar voice.

"I was quite lonely as a child," the voice said. "I . . . hated what I was. I desperately longed to be human, and I was envious of you. You got to live with our mother, you knew your father, and you were so loved by them. My envy was so great that I did not want to watch over you, but I made her a promise. I am glad that I did. I am glad that I came to know you. Sister, you are stronger than most. Do not succumb to the darkness. Do what you do best. Fight, Mina. Fight."

"I never wanted to marry," that first familiar voice spoke again, the one that initially brought me out of the blackness. This time, I willed myself to hold on to it, to use it as an anchor to pull me from this dark abyss. "I could tell that my parents never loved each other, they just did what was required of them. My life was to be dedicated to study, teaching, and scientific experimentation. But then I met you, and everything changed. I . . . I love you so, Mina. Even after you broke my heart, I never stopped. Even when I learned you were engaged to Jonathan. Even after you married him. Even now. I will never stop, though I know that I must love you from afar," the voice continued, now strained with tears. "I love you. Please, come back to me. Come back."

I continued to cling to the voice, and realized that I could now feel. There was a firm grip on my hand, a hot breath close to my ear. I continued to hold onto the sensations, until I could hear the distant rumble of footsteps and voices, birds chirping outside of a window. I felt the cool air of a room, and a dull pain in my wrist, my ribs, my back.

The darkness dissipated, and I opened my eyes.

I was in a hospital room, lying in bed. There were bandages wrapped around my torso beneath my gown, and around my wrist. Abe sat at my bedside, one hand clutching mine, the other hand covering his face as he silently wept.

My senses were no longer heightened. Everything seemed muted now, like vibrant colors reduced to gray. But I felt relief. It meant I was no longer undergoing the transformation, and I was fully human again.

It took great effort, but I managed to squeeze his hand with my own. He stiffened, lowering his hand from his face as his tearful blue eyes met mine.

"Mina," he whispered, the dark shadow lifting from his visage, his eyes going wide with both astonishment and relief.

I managed to give him a shaky smile, and he reached out to pull me into a gentle embrace, weeping openly now. Though my body was still sore and aching, I clung to him, flooded with relief and love. I buried my face in the crook of his neck, breathing him in, grateful to be out of the darkness.

And then the memories of what happened at the estate flashed through my mind. My kukri severing Vlad's head from his body. Ilona's snarl of rage before Abe staked her. Jonathan's still body. Jonathan...

"Jonathan," I rasped abruptly, pulling back.

"He is alive and quite well. He was here earlier," Abe said reassuringly. I closed my eyes, trembling with relief. "I–I should apologize, Mina. We entered the estate too soon and nearly got you both killed. It was my fault; I panicked when I saw that there was a group of vampires with Vlad. Szabina wanted us to hold off."

"You forget that you saved my life. Ilona would have killed me," I whispered, again reaching out to take his hand. "There is no need to apologize. I would have done the same if I feared your life was in danger."

"I have no doubt of that," Abe said, the corners of this mouth twitching with a smile, before he got to his feet, reluctantly releasing my hand. "The doctor should examine you. We told the staff you were both in a carriage accident," he added, lowering his voice. I nodded with implicit understanding; I needed to uphold the lie.

Abe called for the doctor, a young man not much older than me with kind eyes. He allowed Abe to remain at my side as he gave me a cursory exam. He gently explained that after my carriage accident, I had been in a coma for a week. I had a broken wrist, sprained ribs, severe bruising around my throat, and a mild concussion. Severe blood loss caused my coma, and I had received a blood transfusion immediately upon admittance to the hospital.

"It was your husband's suggestion that your friends talk to you in an effort to help pull you out of your coma," the doctor said, gesturing towards Abe with a rueful smile. "I do admit that I was skeptical at first, but it appears he was right. Quite helpful having a doctor for a husband. He would have treated you himself had we allowed it, Missus Harker," he added with a wry smile.

"I am not her husband," Abe politely interjected. "Mina is my dearest friend. The man who was here earlier is her husband."

The doctor flushed and hastily apologized. He completed my exam, informing me that I appeared to be healing well, but he wanted me to remain in the hospital for another day for more rest before they released me.

As soon as the doctor left us alone, I turned to Abe.

"What . . . what happened?" I asked, my voice still raspy.

"We are in a hospital in Essex. We brought you here and told the staff that both you and Jonathan had been in a carriage accident. Jonathan's injuries were not as severe as yours. He had some bruising and blood loss, but he recovered a few days ago. He has been here at your side every day. After your transfusion, the doctor was not able to determine if—or how well—you would recover. I sent for Clara, and she has also been at your side all week. Jonathan, Clara and the others are staying at a nearby inn."

"Vlad and Ilona's bodies," I whispered. "Are they—"

"We burned down the estate with their bodies inside; they all dissolved in the fire. The feral who transformed you is dead as well. You and Jonathan are no longer under the effects of the transformation. Szabina and Anara examined you both when the doctors were not nearby. Seward used his connections at Scotland Yard to have the fire declared an accident. No one outside of our group —except for Clara—knows what really happened."

I leaned back, closing my eyes. I thought I would feel an exuberant joy at the confirmation of Vlad and Ilona's demise. Instead, I felt a growing unease as I recalled Vlad's words. *Even if you had succeeded, this does not end with me.*

"Vlad implied that there were others," I said urgently. "What if—"

"Desperate final words," Abe interrupted, but he avoided my eyes. "I am going to fetch Clara and your husband. Try to rest, Mina. I–I am quite relieved that you are awake."

His behavior towards me was now oddly

restrained and polite. There was no trace of the man who had made a tearful declaration of love only moments earlier.

I absently picked at the meal the nurse brought in after he left me, and I was not aware of how much time had passed until I heard a delighted squeal.

I looked up as Clara hurried into the room. She sat down on the bed and pulled me into a tight embrace, weeping. Gratitude swelled over me, and I was unable to hold back tears of my own. There had been moments during the journey when I had thought I'd never see her again.

"Mina," she whispered tearfully. "Thank God. My prayers've been answered."

She pulled back and proceeded to fuss over me, demanding that I eat all of my food. She informed me that she would make me spend a month in recovery, rather than the two weeks suggested by the doctor, and she would live with me permanently as I did so—*married or not*, she added. She did not inquire about any specifics of the journey, and I suspected that she didn't want to know.

When Jonathan entered moments later, she gave him a warm smile and embrace before leaving us alone.

I took him in as he approached my bed. He still looked quite thin, his eyes shadowed with fatigue, but his color had returned and he looked like himself. He looked human.

He blinked as he returned my visual assessment, as if not quite believing I was truly awake. It wasn't until I gave him a tentative smile and stretched my hand out towards him that he moved forward, taking a seat at my side.

"Darling," he whispered, pulling me into his arms. "I was so frightened. I thought . . ." he trailed off, burying his face in my hair for a lengthy moment.

When he pulled away, he told me that with Abe's help, he had explained away his disappearance to his mother. He informed her that he had a rare illness that he could only receive treatment for outside of England, and he didn't want to worry her. I had learned of his illness after the fact and went after him, and we wed when he feared for his life, but he was cured now. Mary had been so relieved to see him alive and well that she accepted his story without too much question, and merely went silent when he told her of our marriage.

"I cannot tell you how happy I am to be holding you in my arms," he breathed, as he pulled me into his arms once more. "What you did at the estate . . . I am in awe of you, Mina."

He continued to hold me until the nurse entered and told him that I needed to rest. He was reluctant to leave, and gave me a tender kiss on the forehead before finally leaving the room.

In the day that followed, Gabriel, Seward, Anara, and Szabina all came to visit, praising me for my victory in killing Vlad. When I pressed them for news about any more unexplained murders or disappearances around Europe, any hint that a vampire threat still lingered, they simply urged me to focus on my recovery. But behind their warm words and smiles, there was a lingering tension, and I became certain that they were hiding something from me.

AFTER MY RELEASE from the hospital, I was moved back to my home in Highgate instead of Jonathan's. Jonathan insisted that I should recover at my own home in familiar surroundings rather than his, and along with Abe and Gabriel, he dutifully came to visit me daily, despite Clara's insistence that I should not receive visitors until I was fully recovered. Despite her annoyance with the frequent visits, she did seem taken with Gabriel, whose existence she had accepted with surprising alacrity. As I predicted, she was relieved that I had a new family member, even if he was a vampire, and she fussed over him nearly as much as she fussed over me whenever he came to visit.

As I rested at home, I grew increasingly edgy, hungry to know what had happened in the wake of

Vlad's death. Where had his surviving followers gone? Were any of them still in London? Clara waved off my request for newspapers, insisting that I focus on rest, and I wondered if she was hiding something as well.

Two weeks after my return home, when Abe came by for one of his visits, I'd finally had enough. I bluntly asked if he was hiding anything from me.

"Mina," Abe warily replied, avoiding my gaze.

"Abe," I returned, leaning forward to make him look at me. "What is happening?"

"You killed Vlad Draculesti, the Dracula. He had many passionate followers. Until we are certain you are no longer in danger, you will need to have guards. Jonathan has guards as well."

"Guards?" I echoed in disbelief.

"Yes. Vampires," Abe amended. "Gabriel trusts them, as do Anara and Szabina. You have fought alongside them. Do you remember Nikolaus and Kudret?" At my nod, he continued, "Gabriel followed you for years without you noticing. They will be discreet. You will hardly notice them. They have been positioned outside your home ever since your return."

I leaned back against my chair, frowning. The thought of having guards was mildly annoying but not altogether surprising, yet I could not shake the feeling that Abe was still withholding something.

Before I could press him further, Clara entered the drawing room, trailed by Jonathan. Jonathan stiffened as he took us in, but he gave Abe a polite nod.

"I was informing Mina about your guards," Abe said, hastily getting to his feet. "I will take my leave."

He was gone before I could stop him, returning Jonathan's polite nod.

"She needs ta rest, Jonathan," Clara said crossly. "No more visitors, Mina."

I couldn't help but smile at her protectiveness, and she left the room with a scowl. I turned to Jonathan, giving him an apologetic look as he took a seat opposite me.

"I apologize for her. Clara's always been protective. Since I've returned home . . ."

"I have seen it first hand," Jonathan said, returning my amused smile. "She chastised all of us for visiting when you were in your coma, but I understand completely. She loves you. As do I."

His voice was strained, and I studied him closely. His smile was forced, and he held himself with rigid tension.

"Has something happened?" I asked, worried.

"What? No, not at all," Jonathan replied, too quickly. "I–I would love some time alone with you, and it is a lovely day out. Are you well enough to walk?"

"Yes," I said eagerly, my unease dissipating at

the thought of finally being able to leave the house. "But not very far," I amended. "We may need to sneak out. Clara will have a fit at the mere thought of me taking a walk."

Jonathan's eyes twinkled with amusement. He took my hand, exaggeratedly leading me from the drawing room as if he were sneaking me out, and I couldn't hold back my laughter.

Moments later, we were walking through the streets of Highgate, heading towards Waterlow Park. I felt cold stares on my back, and I instinctively stiffened. I glanced behind me, relaxing when I saw my two vampire guards, Nikolaus and Kudret. They gave me subtle nods.

"It will take some time to get used to," Jonathan observed, following my eyes. "I quite enjoy my guards . . . two large and intimidating gentlemen. I'm considering using them to frighten some of my law rivals."

I laughed, and he smiled in return, but it again seemed forced.

"Jonathan," I said, stopping mid stride. "I can tell that something is wrong. Please tell me what it is."

Jonathan did not immediately reply. Instead, he took my hand and led me into the park, where he sat down opposite me on a bench.

"Mina," he said softly, after a long pause. "You don't belong here."

"What do you mean?" I whispered, my entire body going cold.

"What I said on the Orient Express . . . I still believe it to be true. Your place is not here with me. I think we both know that. It's why I was so jealous when I saw you with Van Helsing at the Langham. There was a connection between the two of you that you and I have never shared, despite our love for each other. If I keep you here in London as my wife, you would grow to resent your life, and I would always feel like I was keeping you in a life that you weren't meant for."

"No," I protested, feeling a hot rush of tears. "I meant what I told you on the train. My life is here with you, and—"

"I do love you," he interrupted, his voice wavering now as his eyes swept over my face. "Which is why I'm letting you go. I know you, Mina. More than you realize. You love deeply, and you are so very loyal. You would have stayed by my side for as long as I wished . . . even at the sake of your own true happiness."

"This is nonsense. I did not travel all the way to Transylvania to bring you home, only to lose you again," I cried, blinking back my tears.

"I owe you my life, but I will not hold you in my debt. Search your heart, Mina."

I looked away from him, forcing myself to think of my future in London—to truly think of it. Marrying Jonathan in an official society wedding.

Participating in dinner parties, balls, the Season. Becoming a matriarch with children of my own. All the while wondering in the back of my mind about the path not taken; the life I could have lived. The sting of regret. The ever-present love for Abe lingering in my heart. And then the increasing discontent, the feeling of paralysis, of being trapped in a life I never wanted.

When I looked back at him, my vision was blurred with tears. I tried to speak, but no words came, and Jonathan read in my eyes what I could not bring myself to say aloud.

"There is no need to pretend anymore, Mina."

He pulled me into his arms, and my tears flowed freely as I pressed my face into his chest. Letting go was an odd feeling, like leaping off the edge of a cliff. Beneath my heartache, I felt stirrings of both freedom and loss, excitement and sorrow. Though I loved Jonathan, I would never fit into his world, though I had desperately tried. The beginning of our inevitable end had been the night he was abducted from the Langham, or perhaps even before that, when Abe approached me on the street to tell me that the monster from Transylvania had come to England.

"I love you, Jonathan," I whispered when I pulled back, taking in his handsome features, filing them away for my memories.

"And I you. I release you from this marriage,

Mina. Now that you are free, I want to tell you what the others have been hiding."

Astonishment rendered me still, and my heart did a catapult in my chest.

"Van Helsing wanted me to keep it from you, but you have a right to know, and I know that you've already sensed it."

"What?" I whispered, my throat dry.

16

THE NEXT JOURNEY

The next morning, I awoke with a resolve that I had not felt since Jonathan's abduction. It was barely past dawn when I opened my eyes, but I could already hear the familiar sounds of London waking up. The distant murmur of voices as merchants opened their shops and vendors set up their stalls; the knocker-uppers tapping on windows, rousing my neighbors from their slumber; the carriages clattering noisily through the streets.

I slipped out of bed, remaining in my nightdress as I padded out into the hallway and entered the various rooms of my home. I began with the library, whose oak shelves were overflowing with books, many of which I still had not read. The spacious yet intimate drawing room where I had spent much of my time reading or preparing lesson plans. The dining room where I had once hosted an awkward dinner for Mary and Jonathan. The tiny back kitchen where I often ate dinner with Clara. The two barely used guest rooms that had unfortunately come to serve as storage spaces. And finally, Father's study.

Only weeks ago I had avoided the room, but now I welcomed the memories that swept over me as I entered, moving towards the desk where Father had spent much of his time. I recalled the scientific debates Father, Abe and I had engaged in here, the hours I had spent studying under Father's tutelage or creating drawings for his publications, the quiet times when I would come in to read while he prepared his lessons or graded papers.

Clara found me as I was seated at Father's desk, looking down at an old photograph of my parents and me that he'd kept in one of the drawers.

"Mina?" she asked, frowning as she entered the study. "Heard you movin' about the house. Are you all right?"

I placed the photograph back in the drawer, turning around to meet her eyes. I gave her a sad smile.

"Yes," I replied. "I was just saying goodbye."

Clara stilled, her face draining of color, but she did not look wholly surprised. She moved towards me, and I stood as she reached out to pull me into an embrace.

"My bairn," she sighed. "This is another day I knew would come."

Pulling away from her, I told her what I had learned from Jonathan the day before.

I had sat motionless as he confirmed my suspicions about what the others were hiding from me.

"There have been more abductions in other cities and villages since you killed Vlad. Van Helsing believes that there are more leaders Vlad allied himself with, and they have followers of their own. It appears we have eliminated the threat in London—for now. Vlad's surviving followers have fled. Anara and some of our allies went to their temporary home in Mayfair, but they had all long gone. Van Helsing and the others are presently at Gabriel's home in Thatcham trying to determine who and where the other leaders are. The threat will not be truly over until they're all dead."

I was silent, reeling from his words. My dark fears had turned out to be true. Vlad was only a part of the vampire threat against the human world. I recalled Lucy's words from weeks ago. *One of the Old Families.* There was the Draculesti family that was now no more. But who else was there?

"They expect us to remain in London while they continue the fight. I do belong here . . . but not you, Mina."

He reached out to tilt my stricken face towards

his, placing a gentle kiss on my forehead, and I realized that it was a goodbye kiss. My eyes again filled with tears as I was struck by my shock at his words and my heartache.

"Thank you for telling me," I whispered. He nodded, placing a folded piece of paper into my shaking hands.

"Directions to Gabriel's home. I don't know how much longer they will be there—you should make haste."

We walked back to my home in silence. Once we arrived at my front door, he raised my left hand to his lips, lovingly kissing my knuckles, and I noticed that I still wore my engagement ring, which now seemed obscenely out of place. When he released my hand, I started to slide it off, but he shook his head.

"Promise me that we'll still be in each other's lives. Write to me. Call on me. Please," I whispered.

"Of course," Jonathan replied, reaching out to touch the side of my face with tenderness. "And I shall never forget that I have a life because of you."

I closed my eyes and leaned in to his touch, and we stood quietly for a moment before he withdrew. And then he was gone, descending the stairs and heading down the street with his hands shoved into his pockets, his head lowered, trailed by two large men who I recognized from our group—his vampire guards. I remained on my doorstep, my heart filled with a maelstrom of conflicting emotions—love, sadness, resolve, excitement. I watched him until he disappeared into a cab at the end of the street.

Now, Clara listened intently as I finished recounting what had occurred. She gave me a sympathetic smile, her eyes dropping to my now ringless hand.

"I noticed when you came in yesterday . . . wanted you ta tell me when you were ready. He was not t'man for you, my bairn."

"I thought you liked Jonathan," I said, surprised. "You never raised any objection to our courtship."

"I do. He's a good man. I could tell he loved you 'n you seemed happy. I t'ought by marryin' him you'd stay away from Transylvania 'n out of danger," she said, her eyes twinkling at the irony. "Anyone wit' eyes can see who you should be wit'," she added mischievously.

"Clara—"

"T'at's all I'm going ta say," Clara said, raising up her hands. "Let's get you packed."

"You're not going to try to stop me?" I asked in disbelief. I had braced myself for her protest to my departure.

"You wouldn't listen if I did . . . 'n you have your brother. I like him, even if he is . . . you know," she added hastily.

"I know," I said, giving her an amused smile.

I washed and dressed in a comfortable lavender walking suit, and she helped me pack my trunk before we ate breakfast together. To my surprise, she asked me for details about my journey to Transylvania. I began with Lucy directing us to Transylvania under hypnosis, the attack on the *Demeter*, Arthur's death, the villagers in Holland who helped us, Greta's experiments in Amsterdam, the train derailment, the discovery of Gabriel, meeting Radu and Anara, and the revelations from Szabina about my mother. When I was finished, it took me a moment to realize that my eyes glistened with tears, and Clara reached out to cover my hand with hers.

"My brave bairn," she murmured, her eyes also shimmering with tears.

We sat in silence for a long moment before I told her I needed to make two stops before I left, and she urged me to go, insisting that she would finish the last of my packing.

My first stop was the school. I surprised the teacher who had taken my place, a woman my age with frizzy blonde hair, gentle brown eyes and an amiable nature. She graciously paused her lesson to allow me to bid my students farewell.

Their faces fell at the news of my departure, but one student boldly asked for a final adventure story. I hesitated before glancing at the teacher, who gave me an encouraging nod.

The students listened with wide-eyed attention as I told them an amended version of the tale I told Clara—replacing vampires with wolves, omitting the more violent moments, and changing the names of all involved. When I finished, the silence was deafening.

"Did that really 'appen, Missus?" asked young Isaac Morris, his eyes round.

"Of course it did," I said, giving him a conspiratorial wink. I turned to look at the teacher, who was looking at me with mild disconcertion.

"Take care of them," I said. She blinked and nodded, giving me an assuring smile.

As I left the classroom and headed down the corridor towards the exit, I heard a familiar voice behind me.

"Miss Murray."

I stilled, turning to find Horace waddling towards me with his trademark scowl.

"I overheard you telling the children another one of—"

"There is no need to scold me, Mister Welling. I'm leaving my post."

I initially had no intention of telling him of my resignation in person, and I'd written a letter that was to be sent to him after I departed London. I felt no desire to see the look of pleasure on his face when I resigned, and I was irritated that I would now to be forced to do so.

But Horace stiffened, actually looking disappointed by my news. He must have had the hope of sacking me himself.

"Good," he said. "I would have gladly released you from your post myself. You still violated our agreement by plying the children with another of those nonsensical stories. Therefore, I will have to begin discussions about funding for the class."

"What?" I breathed, horrified.

"You heard me," he said, looking quite pleased by my reaction. "I—"

But he faltered, his eyes straying to something behind me, and I turned.

Nikolaus and Kudret had entered the corridor behind me. Though they were dressed like London gentlemen, there was no denying their otherworldly nature, and they looked like dark avenging angels as they loomed at the end of the corridor. Abe was right; I had almost forgotten that they were shadowing me.

I turned back to face Horace, whose focus remained on the two vampires, looking absolutely terrified.

"Mina," Kudret said from behind me. "Are you all right?"

"What were you saying, Horace?" I asked coolly, struggling to suppress a smile of relief.

"I . . . ah—" he faltered, his eyes still on the vampires behind me. "I wish you the best. Thank . . . thank you for your work here."

"And I thank you," I returned. "I hope not to

hear of anything happening to this class or the students. Otherwise, my friends will be quite upset."

"Of . . . of course not," Horace said, taking a faltering step backwards as Nikolaus and Kudret stepped forward to flank me, never taking their eyes from his pale face.

I thanked them once we left the school, smiling as I recalled the look on Horace's face.

We took the Underground back to Highgate, and I made my way to Highgate Cemetery. Nikolaus and Kudret lingered behind as I walked ahead of them, taking the familiar path to my parents' graves.

I kneeled down in front of their headstones. It was odd visiting here, now that I knew their many secrets. But I no longer felt any bitterness towards them, only a calm acceptance. I understood why they wouldn't want me to know of the hidden world of vampires; it was a world filled with evil and constant danger. But now that I was well aware of it, there would be no going back, and I had been foolish to think otherwise.

I have avenged your deaths, I said silently, reaching out to touch their engraved names. *I understand that you wanted to protect me, but I must prevent more deaths.*

When I returned home, my trunk was completely packed. Clara's eyes brimmed with a fresh wave of tears as we embraced farewell.

"What did you say to Abe when we left the first time?" I asked when I pulled away from her, struck by the memory from weeks ago.

"I told him I know how much he loves you, and ta keep you safe," Clara replied, with a knowing smile.

During the brief train journey to Thatcham, my thoughts drifted to Abe. Abe, who had never been far from my thoughts, even during the years of our separation. Abe, whose voice had brought me back from the brink of death. Abe, whom I loved—whom I had always loved.

When I arrived at Gabriel's home, a sprawling brick farmhouse on the outskirts of Thatcham, Nikolaus and Kudret trailed me inside the unlocked front door. As soon as we entered, I heard the rise of familiar voices from the drawing room at the end of the entrance hall.

"He only wants to go to Amsterdam because his bloody lab is there," Seward was protesting. "We're surrounded by vampires. We don't need any more experiments, Abe. What we need is to find these—"

"That is not why I want to go back," Abe interjected. "Greta has done extensive research in the library, and she has more—"

"She can wire us any information she has," Seward said. "Going back to Amsterdam isn't needed when—"

He fell silent, blinking at me in astonishment

as I entered the large drawing room that was filled with familiar faces. Abe, Seward, Gabriel, Anara, and Szabina. They were all seated in chairs or standing around the unlit fireplace.

At the sight of them, I was filled with warmth. I hadn't realized how much I missed this group of humans and vampires.

The silence stretched as they all took me in, agape. Szabina and Seward slowly broke into broad smiles. Anara remained stoic, though I glimpsed a flicker of pleasure in her eyes. Gabriel frowned with concern, while Abe looked bewildered.

"I suggest we go to Matford," I said calmly. "My father's family has a country home there that was left to him. Do you remember it, Abe? He only used it when he needed time away from London to work on his publications."

My words seemed to tear Abe from his shock, and he lurched to his feet, his eyes straying accusingly towards my guards.

"Yes, I remember, but we are not using it because you are not coming with us. What are you doing here? Where is your husband?"

"He is in London, and I am coming with you," I said. "We can't stay here. It's not safe. Matyas knows of Gabriel, and I have no doubt that he can find out where he lives. The home in Matford can accommodate us before we move on to our next destination. Father kept much of his research there. We know he was researching vampires. There may be something of use to us there."

"No," Abe said. "It is far too dangerous for you to come with us, I have explained why. Vlad's remaining followers will be hunting for you. Surely, your husband does not want you to put—"

"Jonathan and I have ended our marriage," I evenly replied. "He's the one who told me of your plans."

Another silence fell over the group, and they all exchanged uncomfortable looks at my news. A flicker of some emotion I could not identify passed over Abe's face before it was gone again, and he looked away.

"You barely survived your encounter with Vlad and Ilona," Gabriel spoke up, stepping forward. "It's not safe for you to—"

"It's not safe for anyone until we find and kill Vlad's allies," I interrupted.

"Haven't either of you learned?" Seward asked, rising to his feet. "It's best not to argue with Mina when she's made up her mind."

"Thank you, Seward," I said.

"Mina Harker, the infamous killer of the Dracula," Seward continued, giving me a wry smile. "Of course, she can join us."

"Mina *Murray*," Abe corrected him, looking cross. "She just informed us she is no longer married."

"Murray, Harker—doesn't matter. My sentiment still stands. Wouldn't be a proper journey without you, Mina," Seward said, looking at me with unwavering sincerity.

"I wanted to tell you all along," Szabina said, meeting my eyes. "Mina is a part of this," she said, addressing the others. "She has always been a part of this."

"I agree," Anara added, giving me an affirming nod.

Abe and Gabriel were the only ones who still looked turbulent, but I turned my focus to Abe.

"May I speak with you privately?" I asked.

We left the room as everyone's voices again rose in debate, as if I had not interrupted at all. We entered the kitchen directly across the hall, and once we were alone, I closed the gap between us, standing on tiptoe to press my lips against his.

For a moment, he stiffened with surprise, then fervently returned my kiss, his arms encircling my body to hold me close. For the first time since he approached me on the street in the East End, I didn't suppress the rush of love I felt for him, and allowed it to flow through every part of me, like a caged bird finally set free.

When we broke apart, we were breathless, and I remained in the circle of his arms.

"I've been hiding for so long," I whispered. "I heard every word you said when I was coming out of my coma. I love you, Abraham Van Helsing. I've never stopped. Jonathan knew. I think he's always known, even when I didn't allow myself to."

"I thought I had lost you," Abe tremulously replied. "I–I was prepared to live without you. To love you from afar."

"You don't have to. Not anymore. We've lost so much time," I said, with a sharp sting of regret. "I felt so guilty after Father died that I pushed you away."

"It is in the past. There is no need to dwell on regret," he said. He straightened, intently searching my eyes. "Are you prepared to leave your life in London behind? Your students? Clara?" He hesitated, before adding, "Jonathan?"

"Yes," I replied. "My life has never truly been in London . . . I was just hiding there. You forced me out of hiding."

"Me—and vampires," Abe added ruefully, his lips twitching with a smile.

"And vampires," I amended, with a small grin.

His arms tightened around me, and I rested my head against his chest, grateful to share a brief moment of happiness before we returned to the perilous undertaking of saving the human world.

THE NEXT MORNING, as the sun began its leisurely ascent above the horizon, we all mounted the horses in the back stables. The night before, we had finally agreed that my father's home in Matford would indeed be our first destination. Matford was not far from Thatcham, and as there was no direct train connection, we had decided to travel there on horseback.

I was the first to ride my horse out of the stables. The air was much clearer here than in London, and I breathed it in. It was damp with early morning dew, and a slight chill clung to it. My eyes swept over the distant green countryside, periodically dotted by lone farmhouses, illuminated by the slowly rising sun.

Abe and the others trotted out of the stables on their horses, bringing them to a stop alongside mine. I turned to regard our makeshift family of humans and vampires. My gaze lingered on Abe, who gave me an encouraging nod and a loving smile. It was time to leave.

I turned back to face the countryside. Gripping the reins of my horse, I leaned forward to ride away from the farmhouse, with Abe at my side and the others trailing behind us, towards whatever lay ahead.

READ BOOK 3, *REALM OF NIGHT* now. Keep reading for a sneak peek.

REALM OF NIGHT

Mina Murray and her allies take on a dangerous new villain in this thrilling retelling of a classic tale...

Berlin and Paris, 1890. Mina and her allies have destroyed a powerful enemy, but the human world is still in danger from his allies.

From Berlin to Paris, major European cities have begun to fall to their followers.

To spare humanity from the grip of looming darkness, Mina must defeat one of the most powerful creatures in the world...

Start reading now!

REALM OF NIGHT PREVIEW

I was the one who had lured Vlad and Ilona to the estate in Carfax and killed Vlad. I was one of the last descendants of the Ghyslaine family, a family name hated by many vampires to this day. I had gotten into Vlad's mind and killed him...surely I could do the same with Skala.

But I knew Abe and my friends would never allow me to go after him on my own. I thought of Abe's words at Rosalind's estate. *I will always risk my life for you*, he had promised. *Always, my heart.*

My stomach lurched with anxiety at the memory. I would not allow Abe to risk his life.

I excused myself to go to another room we'd reserved, telling them my fatigue had caught up with me. Abe looked pleased that I was getting some rest, and a flicker of guilt darted through me over my lie.

I love you, I thought fervently, as he brushed

my lips with his before I left the room. *I'm doing this for you.*

Once I was alone, I unearthed two more stakes from one of our bags, stuffing them in my bodice and sleeves, along with my kukri.

I peered out the door. The others were in the adjacent room, but the door was closed, and I could hear the low rumble of their voices.

I glanced behind me. I'd changed out of my walking dress and into a fresh one, leaving the old one on the bed, which carried the scent of my sweat. It would give me some time; the vampires would assume I was still inside the room by my lingering scent.

I slipped out the door, hurrying down the stairs. The downstairs dining area was empty, and I left out the front door unnoticed. Out on the street, I immediately found a cab to take me across town.

As the cab clattered into the city, I rehearsed my hastily decided upon plan in my mind. I needed to isolate Skala and get him close to me, close enough to look into his eyes and probe his mind, before staking him through the heart. I calmed myself with the reminder that I'd killed a powerful vampire before, and my experience with the ferals back in England indicated that my ability was still strong. It was just a matter or isolating him, which would take great care.

The cab soon arrived in the Wedding neighborhood, stopping at the far end of Oudenarder street. I scanned the row of buildings; which were all run down and decrepit, wondering which building Skala was in. I would have to bide my time.

The driver turned, giving me an expectant look.

"If I pay you, may I just...sit here for an hour?" I asked, in halting German.

The driver studied me, his gaze sweeping from my face to my dress with suspicion. He likely thought I was a prostitute, though I wasn't dressed the part.

"How much?" he asked.

His eyes went wide at the number I gave, and he nodded in eager agreement, taking the money I handed him before stepping from the cab.

Once I was alone, I sank back in my seat, training my gaze on the row of buildings. I would have to eventually step out and reveal myself, hoping that Skala would be able to scent my blood; a vampire of the Old Families would know I was a Ghyslaine. But I needed him to be alone... my plan wouldn't work if he were with other vampires.

I stiffened when I saw two vampires exit one of the buildings. It was their deathly pale skin, slightly flushed with blood, and their great height that gave them away. My heart began to ricochet in my chest; this must be where Skala was lodged.

The vampires disappeared down the street, and I fought the urge to follow them—they were no doubt in search of fresh human prey. I needed to remain focused on Skala.

Another vampire exited the building once they were gone, and I froze.

I recognized this vampire. Aurel Skala.

He bore the uncommon height and breadth of most vampires. His features were aristocratic; a prominent brow, high cheekbones, and a wide mouth. I thought of Anara's words describing his viciousness. In the flesh, he looked nothing like the monster she'd described. With his flaxen curls and dove grey eyes, he possessed the dark beauty of a fallen angel.

But I knew who he was. What he was. And I was going to kill him.

He turned to head down a small side street only a few yards away. I waited to see if any other vampires would join him, but he was alone, and no other creature exited the building. Perhaps he was going to hunt, like the other two vampires I'd seen. Anara once told me that powerful vampires preferred to hunt alone.

I stepped out of the carriage and hurried after him, maintaining a decent distance as I took out my kukri. If I aimed it perfectly, I could slice his head clean off his shoulders, and hurl my stake into the center of his back, all from a safe distance.

I arrived at the side street. Skala was already

half way down it, his head bowed as he walked. I stopped, angling my kukri.

Focus, I thought. *Focus*.

I raised my kukri, and hurled it through the air.

But Skala whipped around, catching it in his hand by the blade, his palm going crimson with blood as it sank into his skin. His grey eyes focused on mine, and I was hurled against the brick wall behind me, paralyzed.

Skala was before me in an instant, his fangs bared, his eyes completely black with bloodlust as he sank them into my throat, and darkness claimed me.

Start reading now!

ALSO BY LAUREN GOFFIGAN

The Mina Murray Series

The Beast of London

Fortress of Blood

Realm of Night

Mina Murray Complete Series Omnibus: Books 1-3

Greek Goddesses Collection

The Goddess

Medusa

Celtic Queens Collection

The Celtic Queen

The Iron Queen

ABOUT THE AUTHOR

Lauren Goffigan writes rich, character-driven historical fiction and historical fantasy. She enjoys exploring fierce and complex heroes and heroines of the past and bringing them to life in the present.

When not writing, you can find her traveling to places she's never been, reading the latest book which strikes her fancy, or watching a documentary about ancient times. And, of course, daydreaming about the next story she'll tell...

Stay in touch!
laurengoffiganbooks@gmail.com

www.ingramcontent.com/pod-product-compliance
Lightning Source LLC
LaVergne TN
LVHW041915070526
838199LV00051BA/2628